SAM CRESCENT

Evernight Publishing

www.evernightpublishing.com

SAM CRESCENT

DEDICATION

I would like to thank a fellow writer and friend, Delilah Hunt. You helped me to finish this and gave me the encouragement I needed to send it in. My family is always so supportive and obviously without you guys I wouldn't do this. Finally, to the Evernight team. You are all amazing and I hope this is the first book of many.

SAM CRESCENT

BLACKMAILED BY THE BEAST

Unlikely Love, 1

Sam Crescent

Copyright © 2012

Chapter One

Lily Jones glanced down over the gardens, enjoying the view she'd seen for the past twenty-one years of her life. The only piece of furniture destroying the usual perfect scenery was the man who stood off to the side of the pond, currently talking into a mobile phone. God, how she hated him with his money, power, and general attitude of "I own everything and everyone." How could anyone wish to be near him?

Her short conversations with him revolved around the power of money. According to him, every person had his price. Some were harder to find that price than others.

Yeah, he was a good-looking man and filthy rich, but what else was there to Wayne Brown? His jet-black hair had some length to it but didn't obstruct his sight like some men's seemed to. His green eyes were completely out of place against the darkness of his hair. Wayne was tall—he crowded around her when they were next to each other—and always clean-shaven. The main problem was that Wayne knew his effect on the opposite sex, and it made him cocky.

Lily jumped back from the curtain as he glanced up to her window, a smirk on his face. He seemed to look right into her eyes even though she was behind the curtain. The distance was no barrier between them. She saw the mock smile appear on his features, and she cursed herself for the time spent dwelling on why he was there in the first place. Shaking her head against the confusing thoughts, Lily made her way out of the room and down into the comfort of the kitchen.

Tessa, the family cook, had been laid off a few months ago and Lily was grateful she'd started to take cookery classes, otherwise they'd have all been screwed. Her father didn't even know what a kitchen looked like. Her mother refused to break a nail, and her older sister sneered at the slave work. Slave work that kept her well-fed. Unfortunately, feeding them had turned to her. It was not difficult provided they liked the simple dishes she could cook, but they all expected some French masterpiece.

What had happened to their family to fall on such bad times? Lily's birth had been a mistake to the family, as her parents and sister liked to tell her. The money troubles started long before then.

The thoughts depressed her. Lily got up from her knees, smoothed out the creases in her dress, and went down to the kitchen. Dinner would be expected in over an hour, and she'd rather be in the kitchen, with her troubled thoughts, than looking out the window at the man who gave her troubled sleep.

As always, the kitchen was empty, and she got around to prepare the equipment she'd need for dinner. She took the potatoes to the sink full of water. Lily turned to the sink, peeling the dirty potatoes. She jumped out of her skin as Wayne stood on the other side staring in through the window. He smiled and waved at her, and Lily frowned. The blush already spread up to her cheeks from her neck. It was humiliating being affected this way by a man twelve years older than her.

She finished the potatoes and tried not to look out at him. She knew he was still there, could sense him like a second skin. Lily put the peeled and washed potatoes into a sieve and took them to the tabletop in the centre of the room, purposefully showing him her back. She tried to think of good things: walks on the beach, snow at Christmas, twinkling fairy lights. Lily would do anything to take her mind off the man outside.

"What's for dinner?" His deep masculine voice spoke right next to her ear, making her shriek. The potato she'd been about to cut shot across the room.

"You do know it's polite to knock," she said as she retrieved the spud and gave it a good wash.

"You saw me, Lily. I figured you'd heard me." Wayne stood in her space, refusing to move. She placed the spud in with the others and placed them on the hob to boil. "Why are you in the kitchen doing the cooking?"

"Do you want to be fed?" she snapped.

"Where is Tessa, the cook I was promised?" Today she couldn't deal with him. His cologne was strong and far from being unpleasant. Her pussy was already reacting, her cream dripping into her panties. *This is mortifying. No other man can make my body react the way he can.*

"Tessa was laid off, my father said he couldn't afford her anymore." *It's not your sham,* she chanted to herself, and maybe one day she could look back and believe it.

"The cooking fell to you?"

"Obviously." Lily moved away from him to go to the fridge. She got out the mincemeat and the fresh tomatoes she'd picked from the small vegetable garden she maintained. Anything to keep expenses down.

"Your mother or sister?"

Lily laughed, the sound instant, as if his statement had been the most hilarious thing she'd heard. In a way, it was. Trying to imagine the posh, stern women in the kitchen was quite funny. She pictured a caricature of her mother looking at a carrot and wondering what to do with it.

"Ah, there you are." Her older sister, Stephanie, walked in, destroying the image. Lily turned away. The false happiness would make any strong-stomached person want to throw up.

"Why does Lily do all the cooking?" Shocked, Lily looked at Wayne. He seemed to be furious.

"She does it so well." Her sister laughed. She moved closer to run a hand down his chest. Jealousy spiked through Lily, fast and sharp. Not liking the emotion one bit, she turned away and continued to pull stuff out of the fridge.

"You mean, you and the rest can't be bothered, so treat the youngest like a slave." Wayne growled at her sister. Lily was amazed. Every other man who spoke to Stephanie did so with the intention of getting in her bed. Wayne didn't act like that. It was almost as if he regarded her as a pest rather than a potential lover. Biting her lip, Lilly watched him disappear out of the kitchen. The moment he was gone, Stephanie turned all of her malice toward her. Her true character brought to the surface.

"This is your fault, bitch. You've been spreading lies about us, about me."

Lily shook her head. When Stephanie got into one of her rages, she looked ugly from the inside out. "No, I've not said anything," Lily said. Stephanie latched onto her. Her nails cut into her arms. Her skin was delicate and she knew she'd bruise in a few hours from the rough contact.

"He's my meal ticket out of here, away from all of this shit. You ruin anything and I'll make you pay for the rest of your life." Stephanie thrust her away and charged out of the kitchen. Lily cried out as she collapsed against the counter, knocking off the bowl of tomatoes that fell onto the floor. Trying to stem the flow of tears threatening to come up, she moved to the side and chopped onions. If Wayne decided to come back and check on her, she could mask the tears with the onions.

She was the cook, cleaner, and general house staff. Her job was to serve, not to be part of the family. For the longest time, Lily had been the outsider, the youngest born who was more interested in books than fancy parties and boys.

Mum, Dad, and Stephanie were the true family. She just wished she knew what had gone wrong for them to hate her so much—from a young girl to the adult she was now.

****

Wayne watched the sister brutalize Lily. The fears on the young girl's face calling to the protector in him. She didn't deserve this life—to cook, clean, and beg for the little bit of attention they gave her. He made sure Stephanie didn't see him hiding behind the curtain, and for that, he was glad. She would suffer and so would the rest of her family.

He glanced back to look at the girl he'd come to cherish. Wayne had first seen her at a ball. He requested the presence of the Jones family to join him. It was a charity banquet, and Lily had only been nineteen at the time. The moment she entered the great hall, his heart had stopped. For the entire evening, he'd tried to approach her, talk to her. Every time he got close, someone or something got in the way. Eventually he conceded defeat as he watched her leave with her family. Wayne had made it his passion to find out more about the quiet, startling beauty who captured his attention like no other woman.

After so many parties and events, Wayne got the chance to be near Lily to talk, but every conversation ended with talks about money. There was no chance to explore all he wanted to know about her.

Her family's dire situation had come to his attention by accident. He'd overheard a conversation at the bank, and a few discussions with some friends and business associates. There was a hefty sum of money needed to buy their debt, and all he had to do was put the wheels in motion for the Jones family.

Two years on and he had everything he desired at his fingertips: money, power, and the upper hand. He knew Lily's thoughts about him were less than appealing from the way she tried to avoid him, and the expressions on her face gave her away. In fact, she spent most of the time trying to steer clear of him, after today, no more.

Wayne Brown wanted her, and he intended to have her.

Leaving his hiding place, he went in search of Lily's father and mother. George and Jessica Jones should be more than happy with what he had in mind. After all, it was the expected outcome from families within their higher circles. Once the hard times hit, it took George and Jessica Jones years to accept their doomed fate and they continued to spend money they did not have. Families who participated in marriages of convenience, and all that nonsense, expanded their social status.

Their marriage would start out as convenience, but he wanted to ignite and consume the passion he saw sparkle within her. Her own fire needed to be stroked by him and him alone.

Chapter Two

Shepherd's pie, a simple yet truly English dish. Lily held her breath as everyone dived in. Her father glared daggers at her, along with Stephanie and her mother. She didn't have the first clue as to what she'd done wrong, but from the nasty looks, it would leave a bitter taste in anyone's mouth.

"Pass me the wine, Lily," Stephanie demanded. Swallowing against the lump in her throat, she passed the bottle of wine and cringed at the cheap brand. She noticed as Wayne sent a stern look at her family. What had she missed?

"Who taught you to cook?" Wayne interrupted the tense silence. He directed the question at her.

For the past few days, he'd been staying with them. He was the only one who tried to include her in the conversation.

"Why, is it bad?"

"No, it's really good."

"Oh," she whispered. The dinner continued in tense silence until Lily moved to collect the dishes.

"Put those down, Lily. Stephanie can handle those. Would you join me in the study with Wayne and your mother." A command not a question from her father.

"Excuse me, but what am I supposed to do?" Her sister fumed.

"Put them in the sink, add hot water, and rinse them. Easy and simple, so you should enjoy it," Wayne said. He followed behind Lily.

A giggle erupted from Lily before she could stop, and she clamped a hand over her mouth. "Does she even know where the sink is?" he asked, and the giggle came forth once again.

This shouldn't be right. She shouldn't find him funny. She hated him, didn't she? Confused by her own thoughts, she followed the three of them in silence. They entered her father's study. The one place in the house she despised more than any other was her father's study. The room stank of superiority, and it made her stomach turn with sickness. She eased down to sit on the edge of the seat and looked at her father. When she was called to this room, it was usually to receive a punishment for some crime or other she'd committed. Would he punish her for simply breathing? Lily was shocked to see Wayne stand behind her father, staring out of the window. Even her mother stayed clear of the power of the desk. Wayne's lack of fear caused her to relax a little. Only a little. This was her family, and she knew what they were capable of.

"Lily, I don't know if you're aware, but our family has fallen on hard times," her father said. Did the man think she was thick? She may not have attended university like her sister and the rest of them, but she still excelled in school. Cheeky bastard.

The desire to say "well, duh" was strong but she held her tongue. Lily had no desire for Wayne to see the way her father treated her for running her mouth.

"Well, these hard times have come to a head, and Mr. Brown here has offered to help."

"Oh, for fuck sake, she's twenty-one-years-old. She knows what's going on for crying out loud." Wayne turned to the room, glared at her father, scolding the man who still scared her, and then settled his gaze on her. "There's no money. Your father squandered the entire fortune passed down through generations of your family. The house is up for auction. The valuables inside will be pawned, anything to make a profit on this place. To put it frankly, Lily, the amount of debt is higher than anything you own."

Licking her lips, she glanced down at her hands clasped together. The news was worse than anything she could have imagined.

"What will happen?" The sea of uncertainty was unbearable for her to think about.

"You'll be kicked out onto the street. Do you have any work experience?" he asked. Lily shook her head. The only thing she could do was cook. The other thing was for her private pleasure, and no one would take it away from her.

"I figured as such. Anyway, I'll let you continue telling her the outcome, George." Wayne didn't go back to studying the gardens but sat in a chair off to her left. She could see him if she turned her head slightly.

"Wayne has offered us a solution. He'll pay off all of our debts and keep us in a life of reasonable comfort, providing we live within our boundaries."

"Well that's nice," she said. Nothing so wonderful came without a price.

"But there is a condition. A condition that concerns you, Lily." Okay, not the direction she was expecting.

"What can I do?"

"Marriage, Lily."

"What?"

"Wayne will pay all of our debts and write everything off. Our name will remain firm but with the exception of your hand in marriage."

Had she stepped into an alternative universe?

"No, I can't do it."

Lily got up from her chair and moved away from the group. Her hands were shaking. "Can't you just agree to pay the debt, and we'll pay you back?" she asked him.

"How will you do that? With buttons?"

"What you're suggesting is barbaric and old-fashioned." Caged in the tiny study it was getting too much. She ran shaky fingers through her hair.

"There is only one solution here. Marry me and I'll make your life worth living. Don't and I leave today and won't come back," Wayne warned.

"Leave then."

"George, Wayne, leave me alone with my daughter." Jessica stood. The two men looked at the older woman but decided better than to argue. They left the study and once again, Lily was alone with a woman who despised her.

The full accusation of her stare levelled on her. "So you're going to be a selfish bitch once again."

Lily knew this was coming, the hatred for her clearly written on her mother's face. "A selfish bitch?" When have I ever been a selfish bitch?"

"Personally, I think he should have chosen Stephanie. Look at you—fat and ugly—nothing at all like your sister. I can't believe we're being blackmailed for a lesser woman." Each word cut into Lily, but it wasn't anything new. After all, her mother spent a great deal of time over the years telling Lily how much of a disappointment she'd become.

"She can have him. I want nothing to do with him," Lily said each word even though her body told her she lied. Every time he was around, it was as if she felt him deep inside, and she didn't want to let go. Even if she did hate him at times.

Her mother moved next to her. She took Lily's chin in a vicious hold. Some time had passed since the last time she'd been up close to her mother, but she could see the aging take effect, the signs even Botox couldn't hide. "Now listen to me, you little bitch. You'll marry Wayne Brown, and you'll do it with a smile on your face. You'll fuck and play happy family with him. Don't and we'll all be out on our arses. Am I making myself clear?" Tears formed in Lily's eyes, the pressure from her mother's grip started to take hold and hurt. "I didn't hear clearly, Lily Jones. Do I make myself clear?"

"Yes, perfectly," she whispered. Her mother let her go with a shove. Lily fell back and caught herself in time before she hit her face on the floor.

"Hopefully, Wayne will see the disappointment in you and shift his attention to Stephanie. Until then you'll be the picture of acceptance." Her mother sneered and left the room.

Lily touched her face. She felt to see if her mother had broken anything. Once she was sure, Lily slowly got to her feet.

"What are you doing on the floor?" Lily cringed when she heard his voice. Before he turned up, everything was going fine, and now, she was left with nothing but blackmail.

"I think the floor is comfortable." She lied. Nothing about the study gave any indication of comfort.

"Witty comments. I've been told you have an answer for me." Lily stood and put her back to him. She knew from the dull ache near her jaw that the marks would resemble her mother's touch, and like every other time, shame built inside her. She needed to keep the marks hidden. "Look at me, Lily."

"Yes, I'll marry you," she said.

"Turn around, Lily," he repeated his request.

"Why?"

"I want to see the face of the woman I'm going to marry."

Lily took a deep breath before she turned to face him. He gasped, and instantly, her hand went to her face. The marks weren't that bad, surely.

"Why me?" she asked.

The marks didn't matter. What she was going through didn't matter but this did.

"What are you talking about? Who did this to your face?" He came over and reached out to touch her. He didn't lay a finger on her. Her flinch kept him away.

"I'm not Stephanie. You could have any number of girls. Stephanie would be more than willing to be anything you want. Why me? I'm not good—" She stopped, unable to bear the years of hurt brought by the people who were supposed to love her the most. Ironic really, the amount of pain family could produce.

"Stephanie isn't you."

"She's pretty and slim."

"I don't want to fuck a bag of bones."

Lily gasped. His words were crude, vulgar, and strangely erotic. "There is no need for that. I get it. You want me to fuck. Fuck the fat Jones girl, is that it? Take one for the team?" She started to shout, and the tears she'd held in so long suddenly overflowed and poured down her cheeks.

"Don't you dare talk about yourself like that," he growled. Wayne took her in his arms and held her against his chest.

Lily pushed him away, lashing out, and hit him.

"I don't want to marry you. I hate you and everything you stand for. I hate you," she screamed. She raved and through it all, he let her. When she was finished and exhausted, he held her close. No words were spoken.

"You'll marry me because I demand it. One month from today, you'll be at the church where we decide, putting a ring on your finger, and you'll belong to me for better or worse."

"And if I don't?" Lily couldn't believe the rebellion in her. Why was she attacking the man who was prepared to give her the whole world?

"If you don't, I'll make your life and the life of your family a living hell. I'm a beast, Lily. You should have heard about my reputation by now. I take and take and very rarely give. Take this opportunity as the gift that it is."

Yes, she'd heard about his fierce reputation in the boardroom and the bedroom. The Beast with his face like sin, he tempted everyone and everything. Oh, the power and pleasure he could give. What would it feel like to be the one to receive such pleasure? Lily gazed up into his handsome face, struck again by the magnetic green of his eyes. She could sink into their depths without a care in the world. His lips were firm but Lily imagined they held the promise of pleasure and sweetness. The pages in magazines and papers were always prepared to dish out the latest kiss and tell story on Wayne and his current girlfriend. Wayne was built, his muscles showing he didn't spend all of his time behind a desk.

"That's blackmail," she accused. Lily was trapped in a corner, no way to get out. Any other person would tell their family to go fuck themselves after her treatment, but she couldn't do it, couldn't leave her family high and dry after everything. After all the insults and years of torment, she still loved them.

"It's what I call life, sweetheart. And sometimes we have to make decisions we don't like, so deal with it." Wayne threw his hands up in the air and walked away.

"Can't I have time to decide? This is too much to take in."

"You've got until I walk out of the room."

"But that's too soon. I need time to think." Lily moved away and faced the shelves of books. Useless material, her father didn't even know what they possessed.

She jumped when Wayne's hands came down on her shoulders, spinning her around. He pressed against her, trapping her between the wood and the hard length of his body.

"Life is full of hard decisions and now is the time for you to make some, Lily. Will you marry me and save your family along with this mausoleum, or will you reject me and leave your family and yourself to rot?" Lily, about to answer his question, got cut off by the position of his lips on hers in a heart stopping first kiss. Lily gasped. Before she could stop herself, she wrapped her arms around his neck and gave herself over to his ownership. The way her life had been for the last few years, she'd never dated many boys. Interaction of a physical nature always consisted of a peck on the cheek or a brief press of lips. Wayne wasn't a boy but a man. Pure, dominant, and masculine. Lily moaned as his tongue pressed against her lips, seeking entrance. Without question, she opened and when her own tongue met with his, she moaned. His taste erupted on her tongue, coffee and mint exploded inside her mouth. Wayne pressed her up against the shelves. His hands intertwined with hers and locked them above her head.

Lily cried out when he moved away, and his lips travelled down to her neck. He bit into the delicate, sensitive flesh between her ear and collarbone. Heat pooled at her centre, her panties soaked with cream. She screamed as his hand landed at the apex of her thighs through her simple dress.

"You're so fucking wet," he said, and the noise only served to drive her arousal higher.

Taking her lips again, he kissed her, and his hand explored between her legs. Lily knew she should stop his exploration but the part of her that had lay dormant for so many years was awakening. It called out to her to let him do whatever the hell he wanted.

He pulled her summer dress out of the way. She opened her legs, inviting him in, and he pushed aside her flimsy panties. Now Lily truly knew what it was like to have a man between her thighs. His touch burned every part, and she could do nothing but stare into his eyes. One hand still trapped her own above her head, stopping her from moving away from him. She should find her voice and scream at him to back down and leave her alone, but Lily knew she wanted his touch more than she wanted to take her next breath.

"You're burning my hand, so hot and wet." He moaned and took her lips. He seemed addicted to her kisses already. "Tell me what you want?"

"I can't." Lily sobbed. Wayne's fingers teased her swollen nub, and her legs were shaking from keeping them open, unaccustomed to anything he put her through. No man had ever been between her legs, and Wayne was breaking all of her own rules.

"You can tell me to play with your pretty pussy. Tell me to let you come. Tell me you'll marry me."

Lily shook her head. She couldn't do it. Marry a man she didn't even like very much, let alone love. As a young girl, she'd promised herself to never ever allow money and position to get in the way of love. Jessica and George married for money and to further their own situations, and look where it had gotten them. Bitter, twisted, and totally broke.

"Please don't make me do this." she begged. Lily bit down on her lip to stop her calling out. No one would come, and she knew her family had as good as abandoned her, only concerned with their own position.

"You'll be mine, eventually, Lily. Give in and offer yourself to me." To state his point, he fingered her pussy, going from her clit down to the entrance of her cunt.

Pulling one hand free from his hold, she stopped him with a hand at his wrist. "Please don't." If he penetrated her walls, he'd take something from her she wasn't ready to give him—yet.

"Why are you holding back?"

"Because I don't love you." Lily respected him more when he didn't push her hand aside and proceed with his invasion. He moved up, fingering her clit.

"Love is for fairy tales and saints. I don't need your love, just your wedding finger for now."

Wayne sounded so cruel. All of her life she craved the love and affection of her family to no avail. This man—rich, attractive, and sexually willing gave her an offer she really couldn't refuse, but also, one she wanted to turn down with all of her heart. If she gave in and allowed him to marry her, she knew her feelings wouldn't even figure into the equation in the future. Sex, money, and more sex would be on the cards.

How could she live a life without love?

Chapter Three

Wayne saw the conflicting emotions cross her face. He flicked her clit to gain her attention. His dick threatened to burst out of his zipper. He was so hard.

He moved a hand away from the wall, and he placed her free hand over his cock confined to his pants.

"Touch me," he said. Her small hand circled around his cock as much as possible through the trousers. Her gasp made his blood race. Wayne knew from her innocent reactions that she was becoming attracted to him. Her leaking cunt confirmed it. She was so wet and juicy. Her hips were thrusting on his hands trying to get him to play with her nub. Wayne smiled and ran his fingers through her slit, gathering her juice with two of his fingers, and then to shock her a little more, he brought those fingers to his lips and sucked off her cream. Her husky scent teased his nostrils, and he wanted more. He needed to put his face in her cunt and lick her clean. If they were in his own office and not her parents, he'd have her spread over the desk, half-naked and close to her second climax. From her reaction, this place didn't offer her many fun memories.

"You're so big," she mumbled.

Wayne knew then she didn't possess any sexual experience beyond the merest fumble in a car somewhere.

Her innocence astounded him.

"You taste good," he whispered near her ear. His lips locked on the flesh. She bowed to his touch, and Wayne knew he'd found her sweet spot.

Their pants filled the air around them, and he wanted to see her come undone in his arms, to watch the flow of arousal consume her.

"Come for me." His fingers found her swollen clit, and she groaned. Her legs quivered. He supported her with his weight against the bookshelf. His two fingers ran along her slit and clit. "Look at me. I want to see you explode," he said. Her beautiful eyes pierced him with the desperation she must be feeling. "I'll take care of you, baby." Wayne knew more than anything he'd give this girl the world if only she opened up and gave him a tiny piece of herself.

All he wanted was the promise of a future with her.

With a few taps on her clit, Lily came apart within seconds. Her hands on his body squeezed, and her cry of pleasure erupted in the air. Wayne swallowed down her kiss, muffling the sound so no one but he could hear or know what was happening.

What would it be like to have his cock inside her pussy when she contracted around him? Would she get tighter as she thrashed wildly around him? Or would she be peaceful and serene? Either way, Wayne was going to be the one and only man to make her lose total control.

"Give me your answer." He growled, sucking her juice from his fingers.

A nice red blush stained her cheeks and the top of her chest. Wayne desired to pull her gown down and suck on her sweet, hot nipples. How many times had he fantasized about seeing this voluptuous woman naked? Spread before him on the silk sheets of his four-poster bed?

"Please, give me more time?" Her voice quivered, and her body shook. Deep down, he wanted to take her in his arms and protect her from everything threatening to pose harm. He needed to stay strong.

"I want your answer now."

"Please..."

"Now or never, Lily." Wayne pulled away and shut off his emotions.   It was time to think with his head and nothing else. "When I get to the door, I better have your answer. If I leave this room without any answer, the debt collectors will come knocking tomorrow. It's your decision, Lily."

"Why are you doing this to me?"

Wayne caught her face in his palms. He looked deep into her eyes. "Because you're the one that caught my attention."

Without a second look, he walked the short distance to the door, each step like a ticking clock in his mind. Wayne closed his eyes and prayed she wouldn't be stupid. She wouldn't test his resolve. They didn't call him the Beast for nothing.

Hearing her sob caught at his heart, breaking a little at what he was doing. One way or the other, she'd realize he wasn't the monster everyone painted him as.

All families had their secrets and so did he. Scars, physical and emotional, marked him just like her. The desire to look back and promise her it would be all right was so strong that he decided to shut himself off from it all. The man in the boardroom took shit from no one.

The heartbeat in his chest increased in speed, the door got closer with every step he took, and he had no way of seeing what she was doing behind him.

A hand on the doorknob.

This was it. Her last chance to save herself and her family.

Wayne turned the knob slowly, giving her every second chance possible.

A twist, a sob, another twist. So close to being out of the room.

"Please, stop. I'll marry you, please don't leave." Her plea snared him, and he went back to where she stood.

One of her hands was trapped in a tangle of her hair, while the other clutched at her stomach, tears streaming down her face.

If he could still find it in him to cry, he would at this very moment. The euphoria inside him was unlike anything he was used to.

"An excellent answer," he said. He picked her up in his arms and moved out of the room.

"What the hell are you doing?" she asked. Wayne didn't care. He came to the Jones's house with the intent of having this woman. Mission accomplished, he intended to get on with the next stage of his plan. He'd acquired her through blackmail and he would have to use everything at his disposal to show her the man within. He wouldn't quit until everything was bound and legal. Lily wouldn't ever be able to leave him.

"I'm taking you away from here. You're going to be my wife and not be treated like some slave." He kicked the door, and it swung outward. George, Jessica, and Stephanie came running over. He saw them watching. Her father looked shamed and gazed at the floor. Her mother pressed a hand to her heart and smiled, and Stephanie shot daggers at Lily. Wayne saw all the reactions, and he was disgusted with them all.

"Where are you taking her?" Jessica came forward, all motherly pretence included.

"Away from you. You'll be invited to the wedding, but with regards to anything else, you'd better stay away," he warned. "My lawyers will be in contact."

He left them behind. Caring for his woman was now at the forefront of his mind. "You can put me down now," Lily said.

"I like having you in my arms."

"I'm too heavy."

"Is that what they all told you? Nonsense, Lily, I'll carry you whenever I want." He'd carry her over the threshold as a married couple. And he'd do the same on his wedding night when he took her to bed.

Wayne was determined to wait until his wedding night, giving Lily the proper white wedding she deserved, and hopefully, win some brownie points with her.

BLACKMAILED BY THE BEAST

SAM CRESCENT

Chapter Four

Lily watched the passing scenery with half a heart. Wayne, her future husband, carried her all the way to the car and strapped her in. His attentiveness was sweet after the demands he'd made earlier.

With a sigh, she rested her throbbing head against the windowpane. Her life would change forever. Her thighs still ached from having him between them, her pussy and panties soaked from her climax. When she'd awoken this morning, it had never entered her head where the morning would go.

Wayne took her hand, and she wanted to pull away but knew he owned her. She didn't have much of a choice but to do as he said.

"What happens now?" she asked.

"I'm taking you to my apartment in the city. We're going to spend a little time house hunting before we pick a property, and then I'll organize for a wedding planner to come around for you to plan our wedding." He sounded so chirpy.

"What happens to my family?"

"Why do you care about them so much?"

"Because they're still my family, and I love them."

She knew what he was thinking. She still loved them, but they couldn't give two shits about her. Pitiful. The entire situation simply highlighted the fact she would do anything to gain their love and respect.

She continued to watch the flow of trees and houses. She refused to look at him.

"They'll be looked after. The debt will be paid and they'll be given an allowance, but they must keep within their means. I'm not some bank account."

"What happens to my father's companies? And you do sound like a bank account. What makes you think I'm not some gold-thingy or other? I can't remember what you people call them." She knew his business acumen left a lot to be desired but she hoped, in his own way, he would still care about other people and their loyalty to her father's company. She really hoped he cared enough. He'd bought failing businesses and built them back up with the same staff.

"They're still his but my company will be overseeing them, trying to find ways to turn a profit. The term, by the way, is gold-digger." Wayne chuckled. Seconds later, his chuckle turned into laughter.

"Please make sure you don't fire or get rid of any of his staff. They've had a tough couple of years and don't need the fear of unemployment looming over their heads."

"I'll see what I can do."

She couldn't do anything else.

"Why are you laughing at me?"

"You didn't even know what a gold-digger was, so I'm reassured you're not after me for my money."

"The only reason I'm in this car is because of your money."

"No, it's not. You're in this car because you want to protect your family at all costs."

Lily shrugged. She guessed it was true.

They travelled through London traffic, well, more like slowly crawled through the city. Lily saw Wayne getting frustrated. She hated how the man at her side intrigued her. Never before, with any other boy, had her body come alive the way it had with Wayne. But he wasn't a boy, he was a man. A full-blown hard-as-nails man.

Her pussy still throbbed, and an emptiness consumed her. Lily couldn't explain it, but after her climax, she expected more and didn't understand why Wayne hadn't continued. They came to a stop outside a busy and extravagant apartment complex.

"I take it this is yours?"

"Bought it several years ago. It's just easier to come here instead of finding a hotel." He handed his card over to the man waiting outside the doors.

"Good afternoon, Mr. Brown," the man said at the same time as he took his card. Wayne cut the engine, got out, and went to assist Lily.

She smiled because of his attention. After so many years of looking out for herself, his care seemed a little out of place. Nice though it was, it was from the Beast.

Lily didn't get the time to look around. Wayne took her by the arm and led her over to the elevator. Another man stood to greet them. Wayne pushed the highest button and they were moving in no time.

Never before had she travelled with such luxury. Her family hit hard times well over ten years ago.

"Thanks, Fred."

Wayne led her down the hall until he pushed another key in the door of the penthouse suite.

"The richest come here which is why all the security codes and keys," he explained. "Take a look around."

At what?

Lily stared around at the formal apartment, wondering why anyone would live in a place with so much white, black, and chrome.

"What do you think?"

I left my cold, practically auctioned off home for this sterile place that leaves me feeling colder than the North Pole?

"It's lovely."

She folded her arms and walked over to the window, the cerulean sky and setting sun offered the only colour to the room.

"How about a tour?"

This was getting more awkward by the second. She stood in her soon-to-be husband's living quarters, and if anything, she felt she was on the planet Mars.

"Sure."

He showed her the kitchen—again every surface was squeaky-clean, looking more like a featured home than a place someone lived in.

There was an office, living space, and the veranda that had a pool so she didn't have to go and use the public one in the main drag. Every room left her cold, and then he showed her the one bedroom. The master bedroom.

A dominant king-size or was it queen-size? She never could remember which one was larger, sat in pride of place in the centre of the room. A vanity table, chest and drawers, and a few other pieces of furniture were dotted around the room.

"Where's my room?"

"This is it."

"Where's your room?"

Wayne took her hands, and Lily wasn't ready for this.

"We will be married soon and sleeping in the same bed."

Is it possible for the temperature in the room to rise and drop at the same time? Heat gathered in her cheeks as the world fell out of her stomach.

"I can't do that." She pulled her hands out of his grip and moved away, going back to where she started in the centre of his living room. The place was as empty as her thoughts. Strange, even though her mind was a riot of images, they all contained a naked and aroused Wayne.

He wanted to sleep with her? Okay, a little overreaction since she let him finger her pussy, but full-blown sex? No man had been there before. She was a virgin for crying out loud. Surely, he appreciated her need for time to be on her own before he took over everything.

His hands landed on her shoulder, and he spun her around. "Don't ever turn your back on me. I don't like it."

"Oh yeah, what are you going to do about it?" she asked.

The man terrified her in all different ways.

Wayne brought her flush against him. His dick pressed into her stomach. She gasped, unable to move away and not wanting to either. Lily struggled to move out of his hold, but she wasn't strong enough. In the next breath, his fingers latched into the flesh of her ass and rubbed her belly hard over his cock.

"The next time you turn from me, I'll take this sweet ass." He squeezed her large, round butt to get his threat across. "And spank you so damn hard you won't be able to sit down for a week. Imagine the possibilities of having you kneel at my feet."

Holy shit, she was so damn turned on; her clitoris ached to be played with. Lily shook her head. She shouldn't react to the thought of having her butt smacked, should she?

"You can't do that. I'm not some child."

She cried out when he squeezed her ass again, the slight pain doing wonders for her pussy.

"Baby, I know there isn't a thing about you that's a child. But smack this ass, I will." To make his point, he landed a hard slap on her right ass cheek.

Lily gasped, her eyes widening.

He just hit me! Why aren't I mad?

33

She was confused, no man had struck her—besides her father—and instead of being disgusted and upset, Lily wanted him to do it again.

One side of her ass burned, and she wanted to beg him to make the other burn the same.

"Looks like I'll have to find another punishment for you. You like my taps a little too much," he said. Before Lily could protest, his mouth covered hers, and she was once again blown away by the passion present inside this man she didn't know.

Lily moaned when his fingers dug into her hair and pulled her head back. She gasped and opened her mouth. He thrust his tongue inside, and within moments, the simple kiss became hot and searing. Her own hands wrapped around him, pressing him close: her lips danced with his.

Wayne moved away, and she turned in shock. Someone was knocking at the door, and she'd been so consumed with her passion for him up until now she hadn't heard it. When Wayne stepped away, she could think clearly. The bang echoed off the walls of his apartment. Rubbing at her lips, she tried to rid all evidence of his power over her but it only inflamed other parts of her body. She wanted his lips.

Chapter Five

Wayne stared at her turned back. The desire to tell the person at the door to fuck off so he could put Lily over his knee for disobeying him was strong. She needed time but that didn't make it any less frustrating.

He licked his lips, trying to get all the taste for himself while moving to his apartment door. Wayne glanced through the peephole he forced management to install.

Fuck. His lawyer stood on the opposite side.

Running fingers through his hair to compose himself, he willed his arousal to reduce somewhat, and then he opened the door. He signalled for the man to be quiet and let him in to his apartment.

Richard glared at him but kept his mouth shut. About fucking time, the guy did as he was told.

"Lily, I'd like you to meet, Richard, my trusted friend and lawyer."

Richard scoffed but extended his hand out. "He pays me to stay loyal."

"It seems he pays for a lot of things in his life."

Wayne noted her tone and wished Richard wasn't in their company. Lily was close to earning her spanking.

"Well, he certainly has enough to keep things moving. Anyway, I've got matters to discuss so it's a pleasure meeting you."

Lily nodded but steered her attention to Wayne. "May I use the pool?"

Wayne pulled his wallet out of his back pocket. He frowned at her cold attitude towards him. Only moments ago, she'd been smoking in his arms, and he didn't like the quick change within her.

"Take this and buy yourself a costume. There's a store downstairs." He dismissed her and intended to turn his attention to Richard.

"You're sure I won't try to run?" She sneered at his back.

That was it!

"Richard, go to my office. You know where it is." He hesitated for a split second but Richard should know Wayne would never hurt her.

The door clicked shut, and Wayne was on her. He pushed her up against the nearest wall. His feet tapped hers apart, and he pressed his leg up to her sopping pussy. "I don't know what's gotten into you but I don't like it."

"What's not to like?" she asked.

Fucking hell, he loved this woman. Spunk, attitude, kind, and sexy as hell. He would own her before their time was done. Their time being for-fucking-ever.

"I love that sassy mouth, but I think I can put it to better uses like wrapped around my cock." He wanted to turn her on. Wayne saw her eyes dilate, and her breath hitch up a notch.

Bingo.

"I've never done that."

Wayne knew there was a lot she hadn't done, and he looked forward to teach her everything he liked.

He stroked a thumb over her luscious lips and pressed to gain access. "Then that's something we better rectify. I want these lips, red and puffy, swallowing me down." She sucked his thumb like a lollipop and licked along the tip. "You'll be a natural at it."

Wayne may have blackmailed, and in effect bought his future wife, but all the clichés of convenience and having a marriage to carry on the bloodline were fucked up to him. He wanted a full-blown marriage. His biggest problem was his impatience. He couldn't deal with the time it would take to woo her properly and risk never being part of her life at all.

Her eyes opened and she gazed at him, and all he wanted to do was lose himself in her stare. "Go and get a costume while I deal with business. This is your home now, your life. Please, share it with me." That was all he would give her. He'd never begged in his whole life, and he wouldn't start now even if this woman owned his heart and didn't yet know it.

She nodded, and he let her go. At the door, she took a lingering look back at him and then left.

Wayne made his way to his office where he'd sent Richard earlier. Richard sat at the desk drumming his fingers along the hard stained wood. He stood when Wayne entered. "Trusted friend and lawyer? I take it you haven't introduced her to our other friend Tony?"

Tony, Richard, and Wayne had been inseparable as they grew up and when they went to college, they were known as the terrible trio. Other men feared and admired them while women cried for their attention.

Wayne shook his head and went straight for his scotch supply.

"How long has she agreed to be your wife?" He heard the laughter in his friend's voice, but he didn't care. Wayne needed to have the burn of the sharp liquor to know he was still alive after she left his apartment. "So this is the girl you've been following around like a puppy dog?"

"She doesn't know that, and I'd like to keep it that way." Richard and Tony were his closest friends, and they thought he was crazy spending the time waiting for Lily when there was a sea of willing females ready to be anything he wanted.

"She's a little young."

"Don't you think I know that? I feel like I'm corrupting her or something, but she wasn't happy at her parents's place. The fucking place was a mausoleum, and they all hated her. I'm doing the right thing."

"Maybe Lily's a bitch behind closed doors?"

The anger inside him was instant and threatened to spill over. "If you value our friendship, you'll keep your opinion to yourself. She doesn't deserve that, and I won't take it from you about her."

Richard held his hands up in surrender.

Wayne nodded and drank the last remnants of his drink, and he winced. One glass would do. He would never let her see him drunk.

"Please tell me why you've drawn up such a tight-knit prenup? Even I wouldn't sign this, and I drew it up."

"So she can never leave me. No woman would leave her child or anything else stated in there."

With any luck, Lily wouldn't read through the large document tying her to him further. If she did read it, he knew she wouldn't sign it.

"Let's get down to business then."

Wayne sat behind his desk and looked over the files Richard had drawn up for him. Some of it made sense, while the rest sounded a little complicated. He couldn't get her out of his mind, and it affected his ability to work. Wayne heard her come back. He wondered what she'd bought: a bikini or a full costume?

He glanced over at the clock and wanted the meeting over.

"You really don't care what I've got to say, do you?"

"I trust you, Richard. Get it done."

Wayne stood from his seat and left his office.

Chapter Six

The shop downstairs had been packed full of women, and she hated shopping at the best of times. The great relief was when a shop assistant helped her to pick out the simple two-piece suit. Looking at the flimsy garments, she wondered if her splurge should be taken back. Being back in the comfort of his apartment was welcome. She'd never been one for shopping. Having a large figure while size zero women shopped always made her feel like a sore thumb.

Never being a small woman, she knew she wouldn't be on the catwalk anytime soon. Sighing, she pulled off her dress and underwear, stood in front of the mirror to gaze at her reflection. She wondered what Wayne saw in her. Her legs were too large, her hips too wide, belly rounded instead of flat. Her breasts were pert and a handful even to her.

When she was around Wayne, he made her feel small and dainty. No choice left, she put on the deep purple costume. There were ties at one of her hips for the briefs, and she'd need someone to help with the top part. The top consisted of two cups held together by flimsy string. She tied one part around her neck and then moulded the fabric over the large breasts to give her some respect. Why couldn't she have been given a decent pair? Ones that weren't the size of melons. Lily went in search of Wayne to help with the ties.

She walked into the hall and crashed into a hard muscular chest she wasn't accustomed to. Firm hands held her steady.

"I'm so sorry," she said as she looked at Richard. Lily was mortified he'd caught her semi-naked.

"No need to be sorry when a half-naked woman crashes into me."

Wayne came round him, and his gaze skimmed her body. The blush heated her cheeks and chest. She couldn't see it, but she knew it was there.

"I-I...." She stopped and licked her lips. "Could...you...could you please do me up?" She gave him her back and then remembered her ass was on display.

Lily squeaked and spun, the top slipping. A breast popped free. She squealed and ran from the men.

Lily heard them talk, and then seconds later, Wayne was back in his office and he stared at her, amusement shining in his eyes.

"I'm so sorry." Her father, use to call her many names, including an embarrassment, and here she'd proven it. What other woman would go around with the threat of a boob falling out as she did?

"You don't need to apologize. Unless you were intending to sneak away with Richard while my back was turned," he said.

"I guess that was a joke." Wayne put a finger to his lips and shushed her. "Don't tell anyone. You'll spoil my reputation."

Lily couldn't stop her laugh, and before long, she saw him respond in laughter. The laughing was infectious.

"Turn around. I'll tie it up."

"I'm not wanting to swim anymore. I feel like a whale," she complained. Lily shook her head not knowing why she mentioned her insecurity. Most women had weight issues. The women who travelled in Wayne's social circles were notorious for being super slim. The classic size zero.

They'd had a pool at home, and she used to love soaking in the sun and taking a swim. George and Jessica hired a pool boy to clean it, and then Stephanie was out every opportunity to tease her, shooting nasty comments about her size and the way she looked.

Shame when the pool boy laughed at the cruel words. That had been about three years ago, before the staff were let go one by one. She never went into the pool again.

Wayne's hands landed on her hips. "Why do you say awful things about yourself?" he whispered near her ear. His breath disturbed the hair on her neck. Goosebumps erupted on her flesh, and she gasped when his teeth grazed the surface of her skin. Her neck was so sensitive, small touches driving her crazy. She knew from past hairdressing experiences.

He moved from the hips up to her ribs.

"I'm not blind. I know what I look like."

The way he touched her, she was starting to have doubts.

"Do you really?" He continued upwards, the pads of his fingers ran over her breasts.

"We shouldn't be doing this."

"Doing what?"

"You touching me."

"Lily, I'm going to be your husband as soon as it can be arranged. I think touching is permitted." Wayne caressed farther up, sending her arms above her head. He touched her hands before roaming down and wrapped his arms round her stomach. Lily tried to suck in her belly.

"Don't. I love your body, and I want to see it more often. Purple really flatters you." His fingers circled the flesh of her belly.

She let out the breath and leaned back. "Do you feel that?" he asked, and Lily shook her head. Wayne thrust his pelvis against her ass, and Lily jumped. "I want you. I'll always want you."

Turning her, he slammed his mouth over hers. His tongue thrust inside her.

Lily, stunned by the action, didn't respond at first.

"Touch me, Lily. Kiss me." This was the first time she'd heard him command, and she placed her hands on him. "No, touch me here." He took her hand and pressed it over his stiff shaft.

"You're really hard. Does it hurt?"

Wayne chuckled. "Yes, but in a good way."

"I can't do this. I'm not ready."

Sighing, Wayne took a step back. "Go and jump in the pool. I'll be there soon."

Pleased to be out of the way, Lily walked slowly to the door and left for the pool. The setting sun was a beauty to behold. The pool was in a sunroom, providing plenty of protection from the cold air outside.

****

Wayne watched her go, and it seemed he spent most of his time watching her leave. He moved through to the en-suite bathroom and started the shower. He peeled off his clothing and climbed in.

Glancing down, he moaned at the red swollen cock sticking straight out, begging for attention.

He wouldn't be able to go out with the thick erection. Wayne wanted Lily to become accustomed to his presence, not terrified this early on. He reached for the soap and lathered his cock, the bubbles helping him thrust through his fist.

Resting his forehead on his arm on the shower stall, he closed his eyes and imagined Lily coming into the bathroom to meet him. She wore a cute little towel that dropped to the floor when she saw him fucking his own hand. He groaned, wondering what it would feel like to have her naked little fist wrapped around his dick instead of his own hand. The cold water hit his back, but he couldn't feel it. With his eyes closed, he could almost imagine her stood there.

Wayne thought about her lush mouth. The plump lips spread around his aching dick, sucking him into the back of her throat. There was so much to teach her. His cry echoed off the walls of the bathroom as he envisioned her on her knees in front of him, deep-throating his shaft. His thick sperm landed on the tile, and he shook all over from the power of his climax. Wayne prayed he wouldn't be forced to resort to a cold shower and the love of his fist all that often.

He cleaned up his mess and went to get his own swimming trunks. He would join her in the pool and talk. Wayne didn't want a sex object. He wanted a wife, and so far, every touch had resorted in a sexual display of his dominance. All he sought to do was be with her and show her he wasn't all that bad company.

Minutes later, he found her floating in the pool. Wayne stopped and stared. Her eyes were closed, and he couldn't determine if she had a smile on her face or looked sad.

Slowly, so as not to disturb her, he moved to the farthest end of the pool and waited.

SAM CRESCENT

Chapter Seven

Lily knew he was there but didn't know how best to approach him. It was as if he knew every part of her already. Whereas she knew next to nothing about him.

He was cruel and named the "Beast", and from what she'd read, for good reason. A truly callous man, who treated women like casual flings rather than show them respect.

Was that the type of man she wanted to give her virginity to? To spend the rest of her life with him dictating to her?

She kept her eyes closed and soaked up the sun. Autumn and winter were fast approaching, and she looked forward to the chance to decorate and immerse herself in the seasonal spirit.

Excitement built inside her thinking of picking out a tree and then searching for the right turkey. Her family wouldn't be with them for Christmas. They all despised the festive season, preferring the New Year celebrations of drink and partying.

"What are you thinking?" he asked, and Lily knew she couldn't put it off anymore. She turned in the water and walked to where he stood.

"I was thinking about Christmas."

"A little premature, don't you think?"

"I figured as a business man you'd be all over it."

Lily saw him shrug, and she giggled.

"I've got employees to worry about that."

Yes, she imagined he had an employee to worry about every little detail of his life.

"What's going to happen about the wedding?" Lily didn't really care about the wedding. Her ideal marriage would have been to a man she could imagine devoting to, not this man who got off on hurting people, throwing out ultimatums as if he ruled the world.

"Misha is coming tomorrow to talk about it. You and she can organise—"

"I don't want any part in it. Just get her to organize it." Lily knew how harsh she sounded but any protective layer she had left needed to be used to her advantage.

"This is your wedding, and you need to have a say, Lily." He sounded so cross.

Closing her eyes, she moved away and swam. It had been so long since her last bout of freedom in water, and she relished the waves as her arms glided through the water. Her mind was at peace being on her own, no thought of punishment.

Thinking about her wedding, there remained one aspect she wanted to keep to herself—picking out the perfect wedding dress.

"I'll help with the arrangements of the wedding," she said.

Wayne nodded, and for some reason, Lily knew he was glad of her decision.

Maybe she'd be able to come to terms about her predicament.

****

A few hours later, after taking a leisurely meal where they discussed more important topics, Lily couldn't believe how much they had in common. Their political views were the same and they both voted for the same party. They liked similar movies, books, and music.

"You seem surprised?" Wayne chuckled as he drank down another glass of wine. Lily hated the vinegary taste and stuck with juice.

"You like that famous vampire trilogy? Most guys hate the stuff that makes a girl go mushy." Their conversation turned from books to film.

"What can I say, I must be in touch with my feminine side."

Lily laughed. "I don't think anyone would mistake you for being feminine at all."

She picked up a strawberry and bit into the delicious sweet fruit. "I use to grow these in my garden."

"Why did you grow and do all that stuff?"

Lily raised an eyebrow at his ridiculous question. "Wayne, you knew my family's state of affairs. We were broke and anything to keep costs down was paramount in our life."

"If that is so, why were the rest of them still going to restaurants and ordering fine wine?" That was a revelation to her. She prided herself on keeping the shopping bills down, and they still went out and spent what little remained of the money. "I'm sorry I shouldn't have said anything."

Lily shook her head. "No, it's true what they were like. It just shocks me to see how brutal they use to be."

Wayne closed the distance between them, taking the stem out of her hand, and cupped her chin. "You won't have to worry about them anymore."

"You're going to be my white knight?"

"I'll be anything you need."

The intimate atmosphere could be cut with a knife. Lily smiled and instinctively kissed his palm. "I need to sleep."

They'd both showered earlier, and Lily wanted to do nothing more than collapse in the large bed.

"Go and sleep." Lily didn't need to be told twice. She picked up her water and left him.

In no time at all, she lay on the large bed surrounded by silk sheets. She wore an old shirt she'd found in his wardrobe.

After what seemed like a lifetime, she heard him enter, gather his clothing, and leave again. Lily relaxed and sighed, until seconds later, he walked back in and moved straight for the opposite side of the bed.

"What are you doing?" she asked, sitting up.

"I need to sleep as well." Her eyes widened as he opened his dressing gown. Lily slapped a hand over her eyes she tried to cover him from sight.

"You're naked."

"Lily, drop your hand."

She shook her head. Behind her hand, her eyes were closed, and they'd remain closed until he either left the room or covered up.

"Why are you hiding?"

"Would you please put some clothes on?" she asked. Her body flushed.

"No."

"Please." Lily heard some shuffling, and then his hand was removed her own from her face. Refusing to give in, she kept her eyes closed she turned away, scrambling on the sheets, and trying to move away.

He caught her leg and pulled her back to the edge of the bed. Lily fell, and he grabbed her bringing her against his body. She gasped, shocked, and opened her eyes looking down his body. Wayne stood in front of her naked.

"You've never seen a naked man before?"

Lily didn't bother to answer. She couldn't tear her gaze away from him. Swallowed past the lump in her mouth, she continued to plead with him some more.

"No." Wayne was firm.

"A gentleman would."

"I never said I was a gentleman."

His fingers slid to the hem of her shirt. "You can see me, and now I want to see you." In one movement, the shirt was up and over her head leaving her exposed to his eyes. She covered her breasts, and he pulled the hands down at her side.

"You're beautiful, Lily. Never let anyone tell you differently."

Instead of touching or doing anything, he took her hand and brought her to the bed. Turning out the light, he pulled the silk sheets around them. His arm curved round her waist, spooning.

"See, no problem at all," he said.

Lily slowly relaxed against his hold and fell asleep. His throbbing erection pressed between the cheeks of her ass.

Strange, she was comfortable sleeping with a man she barely knew, naked in the same bed, but she wasn't in a house surrounded by her family.

SAM CRESCENT

Chapter Eight

The following weeks went by pretty much uneventfully. Wayne and Lily searched for a house together. All of the styles Wayne picked, Lily hated. While he continued with his never-ending workload, Lily went shopping and tried on wedding dress after wedding dress.

She thought plenty of other brides had a large array of bridesmaids. Stephanie refused when she asked to be her bridesmaid, and so Lily would attend her wedding with the planner as her maid of honour.

In the meantime, they filled their time like any other couple, eating meals in and out. The celebrity world adored Wayne Brown, and Lily had been subjected to an ambush of paparazzi wherever she went.

Her attire always seemed to make some gossip cover somewhere, and questions of Wayne's past conquests were getting tiring. The amount of times she'd heard that she wasn't good enough started to take its toll.

Wayne always insisted they sleep together, and for the most part, he demanded they were both naked.

Her pussy would flood with warmth, and her cheeks would heat with shame. No woman should respond in such a way to man she barely knew.

After a hiatus of civility, Wayne and Lily came to blows over the arrangements of the prenuptial agreement.

Both stood in Richard's office, the document heavy to lift.

"What do you want me to do with it?" she asked. Lily didn't care one iota about the money. As far as she was concerned, when they divorced she wouldn't want a single penny from him or his family.

"You need to read through carefully. If you're not happy with it then let me know so we can organize and change bits."

"I need a lawyer for that?"

"It's all necessary."

"But not completely." Lily turned to Wayne as he said something.

"Why do you want me to sign this?"

Her heart ached. One week left until the wedding. No run through. There'd be a quick church wedding—her dress had been picked, and the flowers sorted.

The ring on her finger was heavy. It hurt to lift the damn engagement ring.

"Can we just get it over and done with?" she asked. Lily rubbed her aching temples.

Richard glanced at Wayne. "What am I missing here?"

"You can sign the document. Just put your trust in me, Lily," Wayne said.

She nibbled her lip and picked up the heavy bundle. Words she never even heard of threw-up all over the page. She couldn't afford a lawyer and didn't want to spend the excess time in another office, waiting for some outcome or another.

Lily took a chance on his good graces. He wanted her to be his wife after all. How bad could it be?

She signed her name along the dotted line, not having the first clue to what she just gave of herself.

Chapter Nine

One week later...

Wayne Brown and Lily Jones's wedding day.

The wedding went off without a hitch—the flowers, the photographer, and cake. Everything was beautiful and sparkling. Wayne stood with one of his friends. He twirled the gold band on his finger, loving the weight and feel of the simple cut piece. A symbol binding him to Lily. Taking another leisurely sip of champagne, his gaze drifted through the crowd searching for her.

Wayne watched her talk with his friends and family, her natural caring nature coming forward and embracing them all.

"I have to say, my friend. You've got a great woman. A little full for my tastes but great nonetheless." Wayne glanced at his lifelong friend and smiled. Tony wasn't known for having any taste in women. If they could spread their legs and get wet, he'd screw them.

"She really is."

"What I don't get is how you managed to get a woman who is still kind and not been jaded by the world. Does she even know your reputation, Beast?"

Wayne knew what he was getting at, and he wouldn't admit he'd used unscrupulous means of which to claim her. Not on their wedding day.

"Her family looks like fucking shrews." Tony joked, and he couldn't help but smile at the death stares they sent out into the crowd.

"The daughter is after some rich meat, so be careful," Wayne warned. Stephanie took great care to try to get him alone. He hated the evil looking bitch and took great care to avoid her.

SAM CRESCENT

"Please. It looks to me like you picked the best of that fucking bunch."

The two men stopped talking when Lily came over to them. Wayne hadn't introduced his best man, worried in case he'd say something to scare her off and back out of their contract. Richard, he knew, would keep his opinion to himself even if he did disapprove of what Wayne was up to.

After Lily signed the pre-nup, Richard wanted nothing to do with him, even avoiding his phone calls. He didn't believe in the tactics Wayne was using.

Thankfully, for his wedding, all the animosity and the trouble had been put to one side. Richard stood with some business associates.

"Tony Welland, I'd like you to meet my wife, Lily Brown." Tony made a great display of taking her hand and kissed her knuckle.

"A rare beauty indeed. How did the Beast manage to get you?"

Wayne tensed, knowing Lily would be uncomfortable by his friend's attention.

"Thank you for your kindness, but I think Wayne gets whatever he wants when he wants." Lily smiled back but blushed, giving away her unease.

"That's true, but be sure, my beauty, whenever he gets out of hand give me a call, and I'll sort him out."

"Before you start in on my wife, I'm going to take her and dance. Come on, baby." Wayne took her shaking hand and escorted her to the still empty dance floor. The music changed the moment they emerged, and the upbeat pop song turned into a slow love tune fit for such an occasion.

Wayne placed a hand on her hip and brought her close against his body. He tried to get her to rest her head on his shoulder, but she wouldn't budge. Hiding his disappointment, he spun them so they wouldn't see her face.

"You look beautiful today." The simple yet elegant dress did her colouring and figure justice. Her mound of dark brown hair was wrapped in a bun, with strands of curls falling around her face.

Make-up was minimal to highlight her beauty rather than obscure it. The small amount of cleavage he saw tempted him.

"Thank you. You look handsome." Wayne noticed she kept turning away from him, glancing out at the crowd.

"Tell me what's on your mind."

He spun her farther away, allowing them some amount of privacy even if they were the centre of attention on this big day.

"I'm just taking the time to process. I'm married, and it's a bit surreal to me. I never imagined—"

She stopped abruptly, biting on her lip. "You never imagined—what? Come on talk to me. I'm your husband now. You can't keep secrets," he teased.

Lily burst out laughing and relaxed in his arms.

"I never thought my marriage would be like this. I mean, it's pitiful. I've got no one." His heart broke for her. When they'd arranged the guest list, the only people she could invite were her family.

"Hey, look at me." He tilted her head back so she stared back at him. "You've got me now."

Lily smiled and placed her head on his shoulder. They danced for the remainder of the night. Neither caring what other people thought.

SAM CRESCENT

Chapter Ten

Lily stood in the middle of her room, rubbing her hands together. She still wore her wedding dress, the reception not giving her any time to change. They weren't having a honeymoon, so it didn't seem right to leave the show only to come back again and dance. Wayne shut and locked the door behind her, and she was grateful to him for shutting the world away.

They may have been living together for a month and sharing a bed, but they'd never shared the full intimacy expected of a man and wife.

"Are you nervous?" he asked, coming to stand in front of her. He removed his tie in the process.

"A little."

"You know I won't hurt you, don't you?"

"I don't know what to expect."

At least she was being honest with him.

"What are you thinking?" she asked. Never knowing what was on his mind was killing her.

"I was thinking about how beautiful you are."

"You don't have to say stuff you don't mean."

Lily bit her lip to keep back her insecurity. After tonight, he would have seen every part of her naked. Would he still want her in the morning?

He took her hand and brought her closer, both hands going up to cup her neck, his thumbs pressed on her chin to tilt her head back. "To me, you're the most beautiful woman in the world."

With the way he said the words, she wanted to believe him.

As if sensing her doubt, his lips brushed along hers.

"I'm going to make love to you and fuck every part of your body, Mrs. Brown." Over the last few weeks Lily knew the more coarse he spoke, the more it turned her on. Hearing what he wanted to do to her drove her crazy with want. "Would you like that? To start off slow and sweet while I take your virginity, and then once I've claimed your cunt and spilled my seed, do you want me to take you again, rougher and harder?"

"What are you doing to me?" she asked.

"Making you my woman." He thrust his tongue between her lips, his hands pulling the pins out of her hair until the mass of brown tumbled down her shoulders.

She closed her eyes, luxuriating in having her hair touched. His fingers ran through her hair, and she held her breath as he followed all the way down to where strands lay across her covered breasts.

Opening her eyes, she was struck by how quickly he could turn her into mush. Already, her legs were shaking and her heart pounding. Her breasts threatened to explode out from the tight corset-style dress.

"What are you thinking?"

Lily bit her lip and twisted to look at the bed. "Will this hurt?"

He cupped her cheek and pressed his head against hers laying a kiss on her lips before he let out a heavy sigh.

"Well, that didn't sound good."

"Lily, you're the first virgin and the only virgin I'll take to my bed. I don't know if it'll hurt, but I can promise you I'll make it feel as good as possible," he tried to reassure her.

"Okay."

Taking a gulp of air, she moved her hair to the side and showed him her back. "Would you help me?"

One by one, the buttons and rope on her corset style dress came undone. She wished she could watch him, but her eyes closed thinking of her mother and sister's advice before she'd left the reception.

He pulled her back to face him and tore the rest of the dress off until she stood in her white thigh-highs and small virginal panties. The dressmaker had insisted on a thong, but she couldn't bring herself to wear something so small. The corset had been designed to not wear a bra. Lily folded her arms over her breasts in an attempt to cover her large breasts. They threatened to spill over, and Wayne pushed her hands away.

"Never cover yourself from me."

With a jerk of the head, she nodded in confirmation, moving her arms down. She fisted her hands at her sides, her nails biting into her palm letting her know what was about to happen was real.

She held her breath, watching him remove his suit jacket followed by the tie. He unbuttoned his shirt and then tossed it away from his body.

Wow! He had hard muscle underneath all of his prim suits, and he had a six pack. Swallowing past the lump in her throat, she quickly glanced away from the hard stomach. A small tuft of hair was peeking out of the top of his pants. Where would the pubic hair lead to?

Wayne took her hand and led her over to the edge of the bed, her heels clicked on the floor. He eased her down and knelt at her feet removing each heel.

"I bet they hurt."

Not as much as other parts of my body.

The stockings joined their other clothes, and he lifted her off the bed and removed her panties. She stood before him naked except for her hair that covered some of her body.

"I never want any of this hair cut off," he told her, pulling back the mass that covered her body.

He pressed her down on the bed, and it was his turn to strip.

Her gaze followed the movement of his hands, and she couldn't stop her fascination. They touched, and she'd seen him before through their time shared becoming acquainted. Now they were married and the simple touch that occurred before suddenly meant so much more to her.

The pants dropped in a heap on the floor, followed by his boxers. Her toes curled, and she clutched the sheet beneath her fingers to stop herself from reaching out and touching. Tonight would see the end of her virginity, and she'd have her long-awaited initiation into womanhood. Who better to teach her than her husband?

"Are you afraid?"

"A little."

"Don't be." He helped her to her feet once again and kissed her. His lips always had the power to take her mind off what she feared, and here was no different. She moaned and pressed her tongue not waiting for him to seek entry anymore.

Wayne pulled away, picked her up, and she squeaked. "You're going to pull a muscle. I'm too big."

"You're light to me, baby, and I love having you in my arms."

He carried her to the bed and placed her in the centre coming down to rest on either side of her. They laid and stared at each other.

"What are you doing?"

"Letting you get accustomed to me."

"I've been sleeping with you in the same bed."

"But tonight you know I'm going to fuck you." Lily jumped when his fingers skimmed up her leg. "See."

Forcing herself to relax, she closed her eyes and gave herself over to the pleasure he was creating.

His fingers caressed her leg, and his tongue bathed her tight areola. Lily arched up to his touch, her breasts tight and hurting from the budding nipple. She cried out.

His fingers slipped through her wet slit, the dusting of hair already soaked from her arousal.

"You want me, baby."

"I always want you," she admitted. The one constant thought had been about this night and what would happen.

He opened her legs and moved between her spread thighs; his wicked intent clear on his face.

Biting her lip, she watched him suck her entire pink bud into his mouth taking the whole of the breast. Biting down slightly before he moved to the next, loving her breasts. Lily couldn't stop herself. Her fingers delved into his thick head of hair, bringing him harder against her breast. Her pussy was on fire wanting to be touched. The wetness slid out and down the crack of her ass.

She moaned as his other hand lightly flicked her clit.

"What are you doing?" She gasped as wave upon wave of pleasure coursed through her entire body. All of her nerve endings stood on end. Her hands fisted and opened, fisted and opened. Her nipples ached from his vigorous attention.

"You're so wet and hot. You're burning my hand." Wayne kissed down her ribcage while he worked her legs wide open.

"What are you doing?" She cried out as his fingers opened her pussy lips wide.

"I've got to taste this sweet nectar. I want you to come for me."

"I don't know how," she said. His face lowered, and she felt his tongue swipe along her clit. The noises were wet, the sound of him slurping her cream echoed off the wall. Lily withered and moaned beneath his pleasurable onslaught of her body.

She grabbed the railing behind her. He threw her legs over his shoulders, his hands going under and cupping her full ass.

His flicks and sucks to her clit were unbearable, the tightening in her stomach making her aware of the upcoming crescendo of passion.

"Come for me. Let me drink you up."

His finger rimmed the darkness of her ass, the taste of the forbidden driving her past her defences.

Lily screamed. Her whole body tensing up as her climax rushed through her like an avalanche in a storm.

She couldn't hear or see anything, the release so intense and consuming.

****

Wayne guided her through, holding her, drinking down her release. While she still pulsed from the waves, he came up to his knees. He pushed open her supple legs, aimed his cock, and looked deep into her eyes as he thrust through her thin barrier and claimed her for his own.

Lily whimpered and struggled around him, but he held her still, not letting her to get away or hurt herself anymore. It broke him inside to give her this small shot of pain, but he had no choice. He was dying inside to be with her. To have her bound absolutely and utterly at his mercy.

"It hurts," she whispered. Tears fell from her eyes, and he kissed them away.

"Just hold still. It'll go away soon." He prayed his words were true. Wayne would never be able to withstand causing her any more pain.

He cared for her too damn much. He'd become a monk before he risked hurting her.

After a few minutes, she started to squirm under him, and with nothing to hold back, he pulled out of her tight, wet heat and thrust slowly back inside.

Lily arched up, her pelvis crushing under his. "It doesn't hurt anymore." She sounded amazed and surprised.

Chuckling, Wayne showed her the power of his lovemaking. His hips swivelled and pushed inside her body, going deeper with each thrust of his body. Her legs opened wide to accept more of him. The Beast within couldn't stop. The drive to fuck her brains out was too much to deny.

Pulling her legs over his arms, he fucked her with a ruthlessness he never thought he possessed. Wayne wanted to make her first time sweet and tender, but the lust consuming him demanded he fuck his way through her body so she'd never forget him. As silly as it sounded, the deeper his cock pressed inside, the closer he hoped to get to her womb. He wanted to force his sperm inside her.

Creating the wonder of life with the woman he truly loved would be the most amazing, wonderful pleasure he'd ever have.

"Oh my God, oh my God." She panted, and Wayne took her lips. He understood her shock and the new pleasure.

Taking one of her hands, he brought her fingers to her clit. "Play with yourself. I want to feel you come around my cock," he growled.

Her little fingers created a rhythm, and he groaned when her pussy started to contract around his hard cock. Already, his balls were filled to bursting with his seed.

"So close, so close," he panted. He wanted to have her flood his cock with her juice before he blew.

Mercifully, she tightened and screamed, her nectar rushing from her body. Seconds later, her pussy gripped him like a fist.

He screamed out as his cum shot out of his body into her. He prayed he'd made her pregnant.

It was his last thought before he collapsed into oblivion.

Chapter Eleven

Lily came awake to the sound of water running. Moving to a sitting position, she released a moan. Everywhere on and inside her body ached. Looking down at her legs and mound, she saw a combination of blood and fluid. Groaning, she shifted to the end of the bed.

The rough sex had really taken it out of her.

Running a finger through her hair, she whimpered when she encountered the mass of knots.

Wayne entered the room, naked, and smiled at her.

For some reason, she really didn't want to see him smile.

"You're sore?"

"No shit." She winced at her own tone.

"I understand." Without any other words, he picked her up off the bed. "I'm ready to serve, m'lady."

Lily laughed, not being able to help it. He sensed her mood but didn't bite, still treating her like a princess.

"Why are you doing this?" she asked as he lowered her into the lavender-scented bubbles in the tub.

"I shouldn't have taken you as roughly as I did. I'm sorry."

He took a sponge and soaped her down. Lily swallowed past the lump in her throat. No one had ever taken the time to care for her before, even when she'd been sick. She'd always counted on herself.

Lily lay and allowed him to care and wash, loving every sensation. Finally, she was washed and clean, and he helped her up and out of the tub. He dried her body and carried her back to their bed before lying down beside her.

"Why aren't you washing?"

"I took the chance while you were sleeping. So tell me, Mrs. Brown, how does it feel to be a woman?" His hand skimmed across her belly.

"I don't know."

"Well, do you feel different?"

"What's with all the questions? Do I feel different to you?"

"No. Nothing has changed."

They were silent for a few seconds.

"Is this supposed to be awkward?" she asked.

"I don't know."

They shared a smile, and she leaned up and kissed him.

"I know I should be hating you right now, but for some reason, I can't think of a good enough reason."

"I saved you from your family. You should love me," he joked. Lily tapped him on the chest.

"It's still family."

"You show more loyalty than they deserve. Do you really think if the roles were reversed, they'd have done everything in their power to save you?"

Lily didn't like to think of the answer. She knew the truth, and it hurt too much to allow her to think about it. It was the very answer that made her wonder if it was the cause of her accepting his marriage proposal? She feared being left alone with her family. Shuddering, she rolled over in the bed, turning away from him.

Whack!

Lily yelped and turned back to look at Wayne.

"Why the hell did you do that?" she asked.

"I told you I'd spank this arse if you ever turned from me again."

"I was going to sleep." She lied.

"No, you were turning from me. I don't like it." He cupped her cheek and brushed a kiss over her lips. She sighed knowing she'd never be able to keep anything from him in the future.

"I was thinking about my family and wondering if there was another reason I accepted this marriage proposal."

"Like getting away from them?"

She nodded. She must be weak to risk being married to a man she didn't like.

"You must hate me."

"No, never could. You're too kind, and one day you'll realize that." He kissed her, and she gave back to him, moaning as his tongue thrust between her lips. Lily didn't think she'd ever get tired of being around this man.

"Speaking of which, I know we didn't arrange for a honeymoon but I was thinking of going away this weekend to the country, maybe making something out of it?"

Lily smiled and hugged him. "I'd love to go to the country."

"I reserved a little country cottage for us to enjoy and get to know one another better."

"You know every time I think I know who you are, you go and surprise me with something like this." She stroked his cheek, pulling her hand away at the last minute. She didn't know what was wrong with her.

"I like you touching me." He took her hand and placed it back on his face.

Lily looked deep into his eyes and was struck by the powerful thought of how easily she could give her heart to this man and love him.

Never before had she been in love, but in that moment, looking into his eyes and seeing another side to the Beast he claimed to be, she wondered if for a split second she could be the woman to love and cherish him for the rest of her life.

Her thoughts scared her, and instead of dwelling on them, she lay down, snuggled against him.

For tonight, she hoped her bad dreams would stay away.

Chapter Twelve

They left early the following morning. Housekeeping had already packed their bags and prepared everything they'd need for their weekend away.

Lily sighed in utter contentment, and Wayne loved hearing the sound of the happiness emanating from his woman.

An early start on Friday meant they would be leaving Sunday night. He'd purposefully booked up to three days off, wanting to spend the excess time with his wife. She looked so dazzling at his side. After a few hours travelling, Lily took a nap while he drove. Wayne had to keep forcing himself to watch the road and not his wife sleep.

Wife? Would he ever get use to the name?

He didn't care. He loved Lily being his wife and soon he hoped she'd be the mother of his children.

They arrived at the country cottage. Lily woke the moment he stopped the car.

"Oh my God!" She gasped, unbuckling her seatbelt before hurrying out the car. "It's gorgeous." She held a gloved hand to her face and released a giggle. "Please tell me this is where we're staying?"

Lily turned her twinkling eyes to him, and Wayne felt his world fall out of his body. She truly was a wonderful person.

"Of course."

Wayne took her hand and led her down the garden path and to the front door. Her excitement grasped him.

Together, they crossed the threshold and explored their dazzling new honeymoon house.

"I love it, Wayne." Lily charged up and kissed him on the cheek before running away and going to the kitchen.

He heard her screams of excitement and chuckled as he closed the door behind him.

"It has a country sink, Wayne."

"So I take it you're not upset we're staying close to home?" he asked.

Lily appeared at the end of the hallway. "No, I don't need to leave my land to be on holiday. This is the type of house I want."

"What, a bungalow?" She went to him, his heart lifted when her arms circled him, and she kissed his lips. Every act she volunteered was a step closer to owning her heart.

"No, this is the type of house I imagined."

"Be a perfect place to raise children," he said.

Lily scoffed and turned from him. "We don't need a house for that."

Wayne frowned. "Why don't we?"

"Because we're not having any children."

Okay, back up a step, his beautiful moment was being trampled on. "What do you mean you won't be having children?"

"Well you didn't marry me for that, did you?"

He needed to take a moment to calm his nerves, the anger was zooming through him, destructive.

"I never once said I didn't want kids and in fact, I do, Lily. Loads of them. I want a house full, and you'll be giving them to me."

For the briefest of moments, silence descended on the bungalow. Wayne was certain he'd be able to hear a pin drop. He waited for the fire to respond.

****

"You've got to be fucking kidding me? You want me to have your child?" Lily couldn't believe what she was hearing. A child—he wanted her to bring a defenceless child into the fold. Was he nuts?

"I did tell you to read the prenuptial agreement you signed. It's all in there."

"That agreement would have took me a lifetime to read. It was so thick I could barely lift it."

"I don't see what the problem is. We've already fucked, and I didn't use any protection. And seeing as I know you're not on the pill—"

"Wait! How do you know I'm not on the fucking pill?" All she wanted to do was have a quiet weekend away without any stress and no worries. She couldn't cope with all the new changes to her life. The huge diamond ring on her finger weighed a ton. If the ring didn't remind her of her now married state then the constant pulse between her thighs was always there. She wanted him all the time. From the short time they'd been together, he'd done nothing but crowd her like some kind of child. Lily felt as if she had no time when she could be by herself.

"Part of the agreement, I got your doctor's forms. I'm your next of kin, and the person who'll take care of you. I take my job seriously."

"That is a breach of privacy. How can you do this to me?" She smacked her chest. Everywhere she turned, he took part of her life from her. What would he want next? Her heart? Her soul?

"I figured in your current position—"

"You mean my family's position. They were the ones to spend the money, not me. I wasn't even born with it. I grew up getting the hand-me-down clothes and the shit life, and yet I'm paying with my life and body and now you want me to give you a child." Throwing her hands up, she went to the window. They hadn't gone away on a honeymoon, but Wayne booked this small cottage for the weekend and when he'd told her it sounded perfect. It seemed more like a way to trap her to turn her into some kind of brood mare.

"I don't want a baby."

"You could already have one."

"You're older than me." Lily wanted anything to fight him with; to get him to back off.

"I've given you everything."

"And took in the process. Don't forget until you came making your demands, I had a life."

"What kind of life was that? One where you scrubbed floors, made dinner, and then took the shit they had to dish out. I may be older, but I've given you more passion than you'd ever hope to get elsewhere." Wayne grew louder and moved closer to her. Lily ended up craning her neck to see him.

Why did he have to be so handsome?

Lily didn't care about his age, and if she was honest, she didn't care about her situation. Her family hated her, and the situation she was in left everything to be desired. A child though was a big step, even for her. At only twenty-one, she wasn't sure if she was ready for such a huge commitment.

"I'm not ready for a child. I can't do that on my own," she whispered. All the time her fears reverted to being alone.

"Baby, I'll never let you be on your own. I'm in this with you till the very end." He took her in his arms and hugged her. Lily held on not knowing what else to do.

She could be carrying their child.

The thought filled her with fear and immense pleasure.

Chapter Thirteen

The weekend went by without another hitch, and Wayne was thankful to the heavens for giving him such a small grace. Lily remained tense around him, but in time, she would come to see he wasn't all that bad.

They made love at every turn, and Lily always found the time to take a shower or a long bath. He knew what she was doing, but all he could do was sit back and watch. Lily was younger than he was. He needed to respect that. He refused to wear a condom. It made him a bastard, but then he lived up to his nickname: *Beast.*

There were times he caught her staring at him. He could sense her attraction. Her feelings were growing toward him but, like always, she'd back off and continue with what she was doing.

It infuriated him. All he needed was time. Time to show her who he really was and time for her to love him.

At the office the following Monday, Tony and Richard waited for him. Both of his friends were becoming the thorn in his side.

"What can I do for you, gentlemen?"

"We're just two men coming to see how married life is treating our friend," Tony said while Richard started laughing, drawing attention from the three waiting women.

"Come into my office."

They all settled in, and his personal assistant brought them each a cup of black coffee.

"I've got the deeds and the documents you need to sign for the house," Richard said.

Wayne took the papers and signed everything before handing it back and sipping his coffee.

"So, how did it go in dream land with the missus," Tony asked.

"Well, besides the little glitch of children being mentioned it went really well." He sipped his coffee thinking about his wife.

"You know it's only a matter of time before she figures out how you screwed her in the contract," Richard warned.

Wayne glared at him. He didn't want to hear about it. He knew his friend disapproved of what he'd done but any other man would have done it in his position, wouldn't they?

"Has she met your family?" Tony asked steering the conversation from the sticky subject of his wife and how tightly bound to him she actually was.

"No, and if I have my way, she never will." His parents lived on a remote island where they couldn't hurt any more people. Consumed by drink and drugs, it was safest to keep them out of the way.

"She'll find out eventually." Richard spoke this time.

"Yeah, and she'll realize the type of monster I truly am, not just some fucked-up Beast people like to call me."

"Don't give us that shit, Wayne. You're nothing like your parents, and besides, you'd never hurt a woman," Tony said.

"Yeah, all the women you've fucked over the years are speaking praises of you. The only bad shit they got to say is you fucked them and then left," Richard added.

Shaking his head, Wayne didn't need to think about this. Their situation was bad enough. There was enough distance between them already, without adding the bleakness of his past.

****

When he got home that night, he looked around and saw how clinical his apartment was.

"Lily, baby?" he called.

"I'm in here," she replied. Wayne walked through to the kitchen to find her whisking up some kind of sauce.

"What are you making?" For the first time in forever, the kitchen smelt heavenly.

"I baked some scones, and I'm beating up the cream. I'm in the mood for some jam as well. Do you want one?"

He found the side counter piled high with the baked goods.

"Are we having a party?"

"No, Mrs. Elliot down the hall is in need of some TLC and company, so I baked extra for her." She sucked her thumb into her mouth licking off the cream.

A bolt of lust shot through his body. He moaned, putting down his keys and briefcase before taking the bowl out of her hands.

"What are you doing?"

"Taking a kiss from my wife." He licked along her lips tasting the sweet cream before he plunged inside her mouth.

Her moans vibrated down to his stiff cock. "I want to fuck you."

She gasped. "I'm never going to get use to that."

"What? Me telling you what I want?"

"That and other things." Her cheeks took on a nice bloom, nothing to do with the beating of cream.

"What about this, could you get used to it?" He pressed his dick against her belly. Her eyes dilated, and he could see her nipples bud through the small flimsy blouse she wore. Staring into her eyes, he leaned down and took the bud underneath the blouse into the heat of his mouth.

"Wayne," she cried. Lily circled her hands around his head, pulling him down to her.

That's it. He needed more. Picking her up, he placed her on the centre table, pushed up her skirt, and tore her panties in the process. The shirt was ripped open, and he placed his finger in the bowl of cream and placed some on each of her nipples.

Lily giggled making the beautiful bounty bounce.

"What are you doing?"

"Eating you."

He licked and sucked the cream from her red nipples. "It's so tasty. Is that vanilla?"

"Y-yes. Vanilla and icing sugar."

"It's tasty, but I want something sweeter." Wayne kissed her on the lips before plunging his finger into her wet cunt.

He unbuckled his belt and released his zipper. He removed his pants and trousers, fisting his free cock.

Wayne licked and sucked her juicy cream, drinking her like a bottle of exquisite champagne. He wanted to fuck her so badly. To take her hard and rough and show her the fire burning inside him.

Wayne couldn't wait any longer. He flicked her clit as he guided his thick prick between her thighs. Her juicy cunt sucked him into her tight heat. He wanted it rough and dirty. To show her how much he desired her.

In one smooth thrust, he plunged inside her to the hilt. He watched her latch onto the edge of the table for support. Taking her hips in his hands, he pushed her all the way off his shaft, watched their combined juices leave a trail before fucking back into her pussy. Wayne didn't let up, but made her take more of him with every thrust.

"Play with yourself," he growled. He'd taught her what to do at the cottage. How to stroke her little bud until she came. Using her thick cream as natural lube made it easy.

They were soaked. Both were so turned on.

"I want to fuck you so bad." Her small fingers teased her swollen clit. He saw it pulse and felt the flutters around his dick.

He cried out, shooting wave upon wave of his sperm inside her body. The pulse of his release sent her over the edge. Both fell back gasping. Wayne took her hand and licked her clean of her essence, moaning, savouring the taste on his tongue.

"Wow." He heard her softly say.

He couldn't agree more.

SAM CRESCENT

Chapter Fourteen

"So, this place is close enough to the city that I can get to my office and make it home every night. Four bedrooms, all with en-suites, and I know you don't want to talk about it, but there is also room to build a nursery if and when we need it." Wayne finished talking and Lily took the time to look around the neglected house.

The plot of land needed work but besides a lick of paint and a few changes, the house was a dream.

"Is this ours?" she asked touching the mahogany stair rail.

"Say the words and it is. If not, I'll put it back on the market again."

"You mean you already bought it?" Lily moved past the hall, looking in each room. Before she would consider moving in, she'd need to clean or have cleaners come and clear out all the dust and cobwebs.

"I saw this place, and it screamed out to me. It hasn't been up very long for sale, and I just got the gut instinct it wouldn't stay on the market that long."

"I agree. This place is a gem." She opened a door into what looked like the home office and closed the door. She glanced into each room, seeing the potential in the property.

"It's so beautiful." Every room she looked in, she fell more and more in love with the place. "We could buy some long corner sofas and sit around the open fire. We'll need to come and have everything cleaned beforehand," she said.

Wayne came up behind her, wrapping his arms around her waist. "Just say the word and it's yours," he whispered in her ear, nuzzling her neck.

Lily giggled, her body responding again to his intimate touch. After the rough tumble on the kitchen table, she thought her body would be spent. If anything, she wanted more of him.

"You smell good."

"Yes."

"Yes, what? Baby."

"I want the house."

He clicked his fingers and handed her the second set of keys. "Have fun decorating, baby."

Wayne pinned her against the wall.

"What are you doing?" she gasped as he pulled up her skirt.

"Christening the house." He nipped her neck and showed her exactly what he meant, taking her against the wall. Wayne showed her the wonders of wearing a skirt with two slits up the side.

****

Lily spent the next few weeks organizing the cleaning and furniture and getting the whole house ready for Christmas. This year would be her first without her parents, and she wanted to make it extra special.

Thinking about the possibility of having a baby, she decided it wouldn't be so bad. She would have a family of her own to love and care about. Smiling, she patted her belly. Was there already a little boy or girl there? After a month of intense planning and changing around of certain rooms, Lily had the home how she wanted. The garden would have to wait for the spring and summer. The grass was cut back, and the trees trimmed, but everything else would be left. She looked forward to delving into creating a safe haven for herself and her future children.

When no one was listening or around, she would allow her other precious secret to unleash as she sang to her heart's content. The only part of herself she could call her own, her music.

She'd had people tell her how wonderful she sounded and even offered to set her up with people who could help. Lily loved to sing, but in truth, she never wanted to do it to make a living.

This was hers and hers alone. She wouldn't share.

They moved in four weeks before Christmas. She said good-bye to his old apartment, and the place she knew in her heart she'd never call home, and began unpacking in their new place.

Wayne and Lily sat eating Chinese food in the living room. Lily had a catalogue open and was looking for Christmas decorations.

"I think purple and silver will look great on a nice natural tree." She handed him the book and took a large portion of soy noodles.

"What about a green and red tree or a red and gold?" he offered.

Lily raised an eyebrow at him. "Okay, I love the look of the silver and purple. Why those colours?"

"They're my favourite."

"Open up." He fed her a piece of chicken, and she passed him some rice. "You did really good with the house."

"Thank you."

Wayne took the container out of her hand. "Before we get too full," he said, leaning over to kiss her.

"You've got that look again," she said.

"What look?"

"Like you want to eat me." Lily touched his face and kissed him back. Whenever he was near, all she wanted to do was love and kiss him. Sighing, she knew in her heart of hearts what her mind had refused to understand.

After everything between them, the blackmail and the baby, the prenuptial agreement, all of it had come and gone, and with it, a piece of herself had gone too. Lily knew slowly but surely, she was falling in love with her husband. Her love was not instant and at first sight but more of an acceptance.

He called to her mind and body. When he wasn't around, she would think about him, miss him. Even now, all she wanted to do was give herself to him. To let him take her and love her back.

Lily refused to say any words. For so long, she'd learned to love no one and expect it from no one. She didn't want to have her heart crushed by him this early in her life. For the time being, she could cope with being his wife with no other thoughts.

"Make love to me," she asked.

Wayne stared at her, and Lily was sure she could sense something beneath him. They looked into each other eyes, neither moving nor breathing. Her words were on the tip of her tongue, but he ran his thumb over her plump lower lip.

She pressed her tongue out, tasting him.

"You're something else," he said, moments before his lips claimed hers, their food forgotten.

Lily kissed him back, moaning with every touch and nip. He bit into her plump bottom lip. Coming away and travelling down to her neck, nipping the curve of her collarbone. Her head fell back, and she let out a moan.

"I want you." He growled lifting her in his arms and carrying her up the stairs. "No complaints of your weight?"

"No, you've got the muscles to carry your wife to bed." She kissed his neck, teasing him the way he did her.

"You're messing with fire," he warned.

"Umm," she teased.

Wayne kicked the master bedroom door open and toppled her on the blankets. They kept their glances connected, and they tore at their own clothes, some ripping in their haste to be together.

Lily waited, lying in the middle of the bed, while he lit some of the candles she'd spread out earlier. His fine naked form was exposed for her to admire. His cock making her laugh as it stood out long and thick in front of him.

"Doesn't it hurt?" she asked, staring at it.

"Only because I want to be inside your sweet pussy so badly." He blew out the piece of paper and came to bed. He stood by the edge fisting his erection.

"Do you like?"

"I've not got many to compare it to."

"Vixen." He caught her ankle and brought her to the edge, picking her up and thrusting her against his body. His fist caught in her hair, bending her back making her open wider for him.

Lust driving her, Lily reached between them and grabbed his erection in her hand. He was so hot and hard she gasped and moaned when he thrust in her fist.

"That's it, baby, touch me," he said.

Lily touched him, kissing him. Wayne fondled her breasts, bringing his lips to flick the tips. He would bend, and she wouldn't be able to reach him.

Wayne toppled her to the bed. Holding her hips, he knelt before her and licked her cunt. She moaned as his wet tongue penetrated her sensitive hole.

"I want to taste you." She groaned as he swiped at her clit.

"What?"

"I want to taste you the same way you're tasting me." She saw her juice glistening on his chin.

"Are you sure?" he asked her after some time passed.

"Yes. I want to give you pleasure the way you do me." Since he started tonguing her slit, she thought about having the hard pressure of him inside her mouth.

He lay on the bed. "I'm yours."

She liked the sound of that way too much.

Smiling wickedly, she straddled his waist and kissed a pathway down his body and back up.

Lily watched him and loved his body, exploring with freedom. His cock lay behind her ass, strong and hot.

"You're driving me crazy."

Chuckling, Lily moved slowly down until her face was level with his hardness.

Taking him in her hand, a blush spread through her body. She was holding his cock in her hand.

"Please, Lily." She loved hearing him beg.

"What do you want me to do?" she asked. Where was all this coming from? Never before had she felt this kind of power, but she wanted to hear his naughty words telling her exactly what he wanted.

The way he grunted and held the blanket, staring at her with lust and fire in his eyes, made her want to be the seductress. To take sex in her own hands and embrace the power she had over him.

Did every woman feel this liberated?

Lily didn't care.

"You know what I want," he said. He reached out to her, but she pulled away.

"No, you don't. Tell me what you want me to do." She moved back between his legs when he reached behind him holding onto the headboard.

"Lily!" he warned.

Blowing on his pubic hair, she turned so her full hair brushed along his body and up.

"Fuck." She heard him cry out. Lily smiled and grasped his cock, flicking her tongue over the head. A salty taste erupted on her tongue.

"Tell me." She came up lifting her hair up and off her face.

"Fuck, Lily." Wayne was fighting, but she refused to be beaten. She wanted to hear his gruff words.

"Say it."

He stared at her and refused, and she wouldn't let it go. Lily decided to tease him. "Say it for me," she begged, licking her lip and reaching between her legs. Her head fell back as she circled her clit, teasing herself.

"Fuck. Lily, suck my cock. Take me in your mouth and suck me," he ordered, and without a second warning, she surrounded the entire head of his cock sucking him into her mouth.

Wayne was long and thick and used all of her mouth. She flicked her tongue over the end of him, sucking down as his pre-cum oozed out.

He swore and cursed but let her love him with her mouth. Lily took him into her throat and back up. Her tongue teased the thick vein, alive and pulsing.

With her hand, she fondled his balls. Wayne watched her, and Lily enjoyed his attention. He cupped a handful of her hair and encouraged her to take more of him, setting a rhythm of thrusting.

"I don't want to lose it down your throat." He pulled on her hair until she had no choice but lift up. "Straddle me." Lily crawled up his body and sat astride his waist. He took his cock in hand and fed it into her greedy cunt. She moaned, loving the control she had.

Wayne smacked her on the ass and began to thrust up to meet her. He guided her on what he liked, and what would bring her the most pleasure, and she let him help. He brought her over him and lifted her up, her legs ached but she tilted her hips down to receive him, crying out as he hit the G-spot deep within her.

His fingers played with her creamy bud as she took them to new heights of pleasure.

"Fuck me, Lily," he said to her over and over again.

She couldn't stop even if she wanted to.

"Take me. All of me."

Their movements became harsher and fiercer each fighting off their own climax until the other saw completion.

"Come for me, baby," he demanded.

"You come for me." She cried out when her own release pulsed through her. Lily ground down on him taking him deeper still. The tightness of her cunt sent him over the edge, and his moan of climax filled the room.

Wayne took her in his arms and eased her down beside him.

"You're so amazing."

Lily sighed in contentment, curling up against his side. She was starting to really love her husband, the man who had blackmailed her.

"Do you like your new house?" Wayne asked sometime later. The candles had died down and they lay in the comfort of each other's arms.

"I love it here." She really did. "I wanted to ask you something."

"What, baby?"

"Stephanie keeps phoning me."

Wayne stopped her with a look, and biting her lip, she waited for his response. "I don't want her in my house."

"But she's my sister."

"She's a manipulating bitch who made your life a misery."

Lily took a breath and stared at the foot of the bed. She shouldn't have said anything. Stephanie always brought the worst out in people, and it would appear Wayne couldn't stand her.

He cupped her cheek and brought her attention back to him. "Don't mistake me for being mean, Lily. I care about you, and I know what a nasty piece of work she can be. I don't want her in our house spitting her lies."

Her heart soared in her chest. He cared, and for now, it would be enough. Snuggled down, she closed her eyes with a smile on her face.

SAM CRESCENT

Chapter Fifteen

"Sir, there's a Miss Jones here to see you." His assistant buzzed him in his office.

Wayne pressed his aching head in his hands and looked at the watch on his wrist. He couldn't deal with this. With it being so close to Christmas, he had plans with Lily. What on Earth could her sister want?

Since her request a few weeks ago, Lily hadn't mentioned her since.

"What does she want?"

"She won't say anything, but she says it has to do with your wife."

Intrigued by anything to do with his wife, he accepted her inside his office.

Seconds later, Stephanie stood smiling at him. She shut the door, and he stood coming around his desk to greet her.

"What can I do for you, Stephanie?" He noticed her attempt at a sultry smile, and he shivered in revulsion. She really thought she was a real beauty that no man could deny. He found her vain and lacking in every department.

"I wanted to see how the honeymoon went. Lily is pretty secretive, and you've been back some time. The rumour mill is circling. You've already put a bun in her large oven."

Wayne stifled the laugh with a cough. He'd ordered Lily to never let her family into his home, but under the laughter, the anger brewed beneath at her cutting remark. Lily was perfect, and her sister wouldn't spoil her new happiness in anyway.

"Well, that's her prerogative, and I'm going to go with her wishes. If we had any news, we would tell people together." Their honeymoon, besides the little argument at the start, had been the best time of his life, and he hoped to repeat it for the rest of his life. Wayne would never allow these people to hurt the woman he loved anymore.

"I suppose it's not great for her. Being cooped up all day in that country house and not even going somewhere special for her honeymoon. I did tell her over the phone it wasn't natural to not go away."

His anger spiked. This spiteful bitch had been on the phone to Lily upsetting her in some way. So the gossip magazines had finally found out about their pride and joy. Sighing, he saw past her fake enquiries for the jealousy it was. Wayne knew Stephanie craved the limelight and to have a meal ticket in a man. He was taken.

Stephanie pulled her coat from her body, and Wayne couldn't believe the audacity of her. She stood before him, naked.

He turned from her, repulsed.

"Come on. I know Lily can't be much for a man like you. I'll do anything you want." Wayne was further disgusted to see she shaved down below. Seriously? What was wrong with a little pubic hair?

Wayne leaned down and grabbed her coat throwing it at her. "I suggest you get out of my office right now."

Stephanie didn't listen, placing the coat on the floor, and walking over to him. His anger rose when she placed her hand over his flaccid cock. If Lily had come into the room, naked and prepared to do the dirty with him, he'd be as hard as rock. The sister was nothing but repulsion to him.

"I don't get it. Why aren't you hard?" She pouted.

Women like her really made him sick. Treating her sister like dirt and then attempting to steal the husband. She had another thing coming. Removing her hand, he gripped her wrist and led her to her coat. He placed it on her shoulders and then escorted her to his door.

"For future reference, if you come here like that again, the cozy little allowance you've been living with will be stopped."

She gasped and spun to glare at him. "Most men would fall at my feet to have a shot at me."

"I'm not most men."

"Well, you must be to find my fat sister attractive. Or does the little innocent girl routine really do it for you?"

Wayne knew he should never have allowed her in his office. Growling, he threw her out, glaring until she left. He knew she'd cause trouble for him. He had to wait until she struck first. Wayne wasn't a stupid man, and Stephanie would elaborate on this interlude, making it everything it wasn't.

Whatever happened, whatever Stephanie tried to do, would hurt Lily. She was already insecure about her body and her looks. Shaking his head, he warned his assistant never to allow her anywhere near him before going back into his office.

After what had taken place, he wanted to get home and enjoy the comfort of his wife. Her love and care.

****

Wayne smiled as he closed the door to his home, the decorative garland lighting up his world more than it should. Christmas, who'd have thought he'd look forward to the festive time of the year. This year had come around so fast.

He'd offered to take them both away to sunshine, but Lily was having none of it. Lily told their housekeeper, Mary, she'd be cooking Christmas dinner if Mary wanted to join them. Everyone who knew Lily loved her instantly, and the love he had for her even before he met her was off the charts.

Placing the keys on the hook she'd forced him to put up, he went in search of her. Music was playing in the distance, the soft melody of love songs rather than Christmas carols surprised him, but he also knew how much she loved to listen to music.

In no time at all, he found her, and he stood watching her hang decorations on the tree. Due to the size of the tree, she balanced on the stairs.

His heart constricted in his throat at the threat of her falling. Frowning, Wayne listened as the words suddenly stopped on the music, but the music continued to play. Lily turned on the stairs, and he watched her open her mouth, and the most beautiful sound came out.

Lily Jones could sing like an angel, and it was natural. He heard the track change and watched as she sang the words. She sounded beautiful and danced on the stairs, propped up to help her with the decorations. The passion and love clear on her face.

How hadn't he heard this before? Her arm swung out for a long pitched note and goose bumps erupted on his arms.

Talented.

Wayne opened the door, and she stopped immediately, coming down the ladder and running into his arms.

He caught her up and took her face between his palms, kissing her.

"Why didn't you tell me?" He laughed laying kisses over her face.

"Tell you what?" A blush stained her cheeks, and she avoided eye contact.

"You sound wonderful. Why aren't you trying to get a record deal or anything?" He kissed her again.

Lily pulled away from him, shaking her head. "I don't want that, Wayne." She moved to the stereo and turned the music off, folding her arms over her stomach.

Wayne couldn't believe what he was seeing. Her voice the most amazing sound he'd ever heard.

"What do you mean? You sound fucking fantastic."

"I don't care. Yes, I love singing, but I don't want to do it." She went back to the tree and started placing the purple tinsel round the base.

"But you could be a fucking superstar." He heard her sigh and saw the frown, and he couldn't understand it. People were out trying to chase the chance of stardom and before him stood a woman who could have it in a blink of an eye. He knew people looking for the next big thing. He could certainly help her. "Is this fear of rejection?" He knew her fear after spending a short amount of time with her family. Anyone would lose the self-worth from them.

After all of her family problems and what she'd admitted to, he knew she was still raw and tender about family life.

"No. I just don't want it. Why can't you drop it?"

"Because you're that good. Why not use your talent?"

"Wayne. I know I can sing, and I know people out there would take me on, but I don't want it—ever. When I started to sing, it was for me, and that's how it will stay. A career in singing isn't what I want from life."

Lily added another layer of tinsel, and Wayne watched her, astounded. Everyone he came across used everything at their disposal to make it quick and make it big. Here stood the most amazing potential, and she didn't want to use it.

"What do you want from life?"

She sighed and spun back to face him. "I want this, a family. For years, it's all I could dream about. I like singing, but I'd love to have a family of my own. Children I can love and spend my time with. Can't you understand that?" Wayne saw the tears gather in her eyes and knew he wanted her to have everything she wished.

He went to her, kissing her on the lips. "I understand, baby. But I want some private sessions of you singing for me."

"I promise." She placed her head on his chest.

"Since when did you want those babies? Not long ago, you were ranting and raving at me because of my demands." Wayne loved the thought of Lily being heavy with his child and the sooner she was with child, the better.

"I've had the time to get used to it, and I'd love children of my own."

"How about we start on making those babies?" Every time she was close, his cock stirred and now wasn't any different.

"I thought you'd never ask."

Her dress fell in a heap on the floor, and she stood before him, naked, beautiful, and willing to do anything he wanted. "How do you want me?"

Her smile lit up her whole face, and he knew he was a goner.

Tearing at his jacket and not caring if it ripped, he tore the clothes from his body and pressed her close. He collapsed on the sofa. She straddled his hips, and he took her lips while his hands delved between her legs, his fingers running through her creamy clit, preparing her, making sure she was ready for his dick.

Wayne didn't have the time for foreplay, his dick threatening to spill over her flush body. She soaked his hand with her dripping pussy, and he pushed his own weeping cock between her lips and thrust inside her tight pulsing channel. They gasped. Lily wrapped her hands around his neck. He removed his hand from between them, his cock halfway inside her already. Lily sucked him in, and he groaned, his hands going for her hips. He held the flesh in his hands and moaned. Wayne loved that there was something to hold onto.

"Ride me, baby."

Lily sat down, taking all of him to the hilt inside her. Her head flung back. Her tits pushed up, her nipples pointing at him. Wayne couldn't resist. He licked at the beaded nipples and sucked her into his mouth.

She screamed, and he helped guide her over him. Using his hands, he lifted her up. He saw where they were joined before he slammed her down, and he thrust up to meet her. She cried out and again they moved, fucking hard and fast. Wayne didn't let up on his attention. Perspiration dotted their skin.

"Harder, ride me harder," he said. The need to come inside her built with every grinding thrust.

"Please." She begged for help.

Wayne moved one hand from her hips, licked his fingers, and pressed it to her swollen clit.

He could tell she was close. She thrashed on him, her pussy getting wetter around his thick cock inside her.

"Fuck. You like that, honey."

She panted and moaned. It wouldn't take her long to come, and he couldn't wait any longer. Wayne toyed with her clit, not bothering to draw it out. He knew how desperate she was. The stirring of orgasm approached, and he saw her tightening belly and the shaking of her legs. Her pussy clenched him like a vice, and seconds later, her flood of release warmed his cock inside her pussy. Her scream echoed around the walls followed closely with his cry of release. His sperm drove up through his shaft and splashed her womb.

Wayne prayed she would become pregnant. He hoped she would. In the meantime, he'd talk to a few of his business associates.

SAM CRESCENT

Chapter Sixteen

Lily collapsed with a contented smile. Her legs ached, and they were both sticky, but she liked resting with him inside her. Nerves shattered. Pulses pounded. She lay with him.

"I've got to finish my tree," she whispered not wanting to leave his side.

"What else could you possibly have to do?"

Lily giggled, got up from her snugly position, and switched the light out before going back and turning on the tree. "Now, it's done." The white lights twinkled, and Lily went back to the comfort of his arms.

Wayne accepted her and kissed her on the head. "It looks beautiful."

"Well, while you're earning millions in your office, I'm making Christmas all special for us."

"I've got you, angel. I don't need anything else to make it special." Lily smiled, her heart catching. The desire to rush and tell him how she felt was so close on her tongue, but she couldn't bring herself to speak the words that would change her life forever.

How had it happened? How had she fallen in love with a man known to many as the *Beast?* Lily didn't know, but somehow it happened, and all she could do was wait for the right time to tell him.

The following few days went by uneventfully. Lily ordered some presents for her family and Wayne, but what did you get a man who had everything?

She settled on a new pen signed with his name. A week before Christmas, she was pulling in the shopping. She'd settled on a frozen turkey rather than risk waiting to order one. It was too late in the ordering season, so she wouldn't get a decent bird anyway. Lily frowned seeing a van and Wayne's car in the driveway. Ignoring the shopping in the back, she put her car into park and went in search of the problem.

****

"What the hell have you done?" she screamed. The pain inside her, breaking her heart and soul.

Men with music contracts and bands and shit stood and watched her having a complete melt down. Lily couldn't cope. She struggled to breathe against the feeling of being trapped.

Wayne took her by the elbow and led her away from their prying eyes and into the privacy of his study, the same study she'd decorated over a week ago. The same study where he'd taken her, made love, and forever cemented his way into her life and heart. He was about burst her euphoric bubble.

"What's wrong?" he asked, folding his arms over his chest and doing his businessman face.

No, she wasn't having any of it.

"Those men, I want them out of my house." Lily pointed at the closed door.

"Why? You've got a beautiful voice—"

"Exactly. It's my voice. One I can choose to share with whomever I like or not. I'm not doing it, Wayne."

"This is ridiculous." He grabbed her arm and pulled her to the door. "You have real talent, and I'm not letting you squander it."

"Let me go!" Lily turned in his arms and slapped him full across the face. His betrayal and the pain inside was too much for her to deal with. Wayne let her go and placed a hand against his cheek. She could see he was angry. He did nothing except look at her. "I told you my singing was for me and no one else."

"I wanted you to share it with the world."

"Either get rid of them, or I'm leaving."

"I don't do ultimatums."

"And I no longer take orders from people who don't know me."

They stood off, neither moving, but the tension could be cut with a knife. Lily knew she looked a mess, her eyes red and puffy, nose running, but she didn't care.

"I can't just get rid of them."

"You don't get it, Wayne. I won't sing for anyone else but me, and I see it was a mistake to even let you in. I was fucking stupid to think you'd leave it all alone."

"For God's sake, Lily. Singing is a fantastic career choice, an opportunity for you to really shine."

"Why? Do I embarrass you? Does my lack of ambition make you the laughing stock of all your posh political parties?"

"Stop it."

"No. I told you what I wanted. You asked me so many times what I wanted out of life, what I craved. All I want is a family and now that isn't good enough for you?" With every passing word, the tears gathered, and the pain increased.

"I never said that."

"But it's what you're thinking, right?"

Wayne was interrupted by a knock on the door. He went to answer it, and Lily turned away from him, not wanting to see who was behind the wood.

"Hiya, Wayne. I really got to get moving so if she could just come and sing."

"No, there'll be no singing," Lily spun and shouted at the man.

"Just give me a minute. She'll be out in a minute." He sounded so assured in his ability to change her mind that Lily was astounded by him. After what she said moments ago, he was still determined to change her mind.

No. No more would she be told what to do or how to live her life.

Their wedding photo on the ledge above the fire caught her attention. Moving toward the picture in the silver plated frame, Lily ran her thumb along her laughing face. Wayne looked down on her, with a smile.

What was he thinking? Feeling?

It didn't matter. Nothing mattered? Without thinking, Lily hurled the picture at the wall just off from his head. The sound of the glass shattering and the frame falling to the floor caused both men to turn and stare at her. Perfect, she gotten their attention.

"I said no," she calmly said, walking toward them.

Lily glanced at the man and then at her husband and pushed past them to leave the room. Placing the envelope on the dresser in the hall as Wayne and the man in charge with the music contracts followed her. "Happy Christmas," she said to her husband, taking the keys from the hook as she left.

Wayne followed her, as she knew he would. Lily knew Wayne wouldn't be able to resist and demand to have control with the final word.

"Where are you going?" He spun her around and pressed her against the car. Any other time, she'd be aroused. If anything, she felt empty.

"I told you I was leaving." She pushed him away and got in the car.

Lily started the engine and drove out of the drive. She chanted to herself that what she was doing was the right thing.

Tears misted her eyes, and she didn't watch what she was doing, going round a curve, and then through town. She stopped the car to get out and clear her thoughts. Her grief was so bad. Darkness claimed her as someone shouted from across the road.

Chapter Seventeen

Wayne did nothing to stop her from leaving. He glanced at the man he'd contacted to try and get his wife's voice onto a tape or a demo. He'd do anything to make his wife happy. How could she even think he was ashamed of her?

"Take your men and get out," he growled. Out of all the responses he'd expected, the ultimatum had been the least of his worries. Gratitude, love, possibly even a little bit of lust, but his plan had backfired. All he wanted was for her to tell him she loved him. Once or twice, he'd been sure she was on the verge of telling him, but she would always stop and look away.

Running his fingers rapidly through his hair, he walked over to his liquor collection and poured himself a healthy shot. He downed the dark burning liquid in one gulp, pouring another glass and then another before glancing up in the mirror and finding the Beast staring back at him.

Wayne couldn't handle it anymore. His wife had walked out. Broken-hearted, and instead of running after her, he was drowning his sorrows. *She's too good for you.* Plagues of the past came to haunt him. The heel of a boot landing on his back, the sharp sting of a slap across the face, the snap of a belt. The people who were supposed to love him had turned him into the man he was today: a vicious, blackmailing monster.

Lily never got a chance with him. He'd taken her from her home, stolen her virginity, and almost took her voice away. What kind of person did that?

With a cry, he threw the glass at his reflection. Growling after the surge of violence didn't help. He upturned the table holding the potent liquid. Nothing went untouched in his rampage to destruction.

Glass smashed. Picture frames crushed. The computer on his desk landed on the floor, not surviving the fall.

The rage he kept contained for so long unleashed. All the anger from being an abused little boy to growing up as a man closed off from his emotions came storming out. He couldn't even tell the woman he loved how much he loved her, the anger at himself unleashed. Crushing the angel he loved by his own need to take.

He lifted the handcrafted vase in his hand, prepared to smash the small trinket she'd made for him. The final part in his need to destroy all love and connection with Lily. Until their wedding photo twinkled from the broken picture frame on the floor.

Wayne glanced at the picture to the vase in his hands, and he slumped to the floor, cradling the vase against his chest, trying to protect the small treasure of hope.

"What have I done?" he asked.

Mindless of the slithers of glass, he picked up the photo and sat with his back against the wall.

Lily smiled out at the camera, and Wayne too busy gazing at his wife to care about glancing at the camera. Lily and her smile held his attention.

In all the time they'd been together he could have spoken the three simple words "I love you," but for some reason he'd kept them back afraid to let himself go.

Running his thumb along her beautiful face, he began to cry. The woman he loved was gone, and it was all his fault.

The despair clawed at him making him immobile. He sat in the spot staring at her photo and hugged the vase until the sun went down.

The distant ringing of the telephone alerted him to the passing of time. Getting up from his spot, he went and answered the phone.

"Hello," he muttered, his voice hoarse from the crying.

"Is this Mr. Brown? Mr. Wayne Brown?"

"Yes."

"Hi, I'm Denise Sutton from the community hospital. We've got a Mrs. Lily Brown here, and we need you to come down right away."

His heart dropped out of his chest. Wayne held the phone tighter; praying with all of his might there was nothing seriously wrong with her.

****

Wayne looked at his wife in the hospital bed, and he wanted to throw up. She'd been attacked on the street with a knife and knocked to the ground. His fingers curled around the metal bedpost.

Tony coughed making him aware of his presence, and Richard followed close behind him.

"We came as soon as we heard. How is she?" Tony asked.

Wayne nodded at both men and then turned his attention back to his wife—pale, unconscious, and in danger of never waking up. Stress, the doctor had said. Too much too soon and his delicate wife couldn't handle the stress, and her body conked out to help her deal. A small nick on her cheek, the only indication of the attack of the knife but the lump on her head and the black eye was evidence of something much worse. Once the man punched her to the floor, she'd been too weak to defend herself. Wayne was thankful the thug hadn't caused any more damage to her after she went down. He was told the only thing missing had been her car. Wayne couldn't believe it, Lily attacked for her car.

"She's doing okay. They keep checking but it's just a case of waiting for her to wake up." No matter how long he sat and stared, she didn't move or make any sound she could hear him.

"What happened?"

"The police said it was some random attack. Took a knife to her and then punched her to the floor." The police had told him they had a suspect in custody from the few eyewitness reports but they needed Lily to confirm identity of her attacker.

"What kind of animal would hit a woman?" Richard growled in disgust, and Wayne couldn't agree more. If he found the guy before the police, he wouldn't leave him alive.

"She's pregnant. They reckon she's over two months pregnant, give or take." The doctor had given him the news. What was he supposed to do? Laugh? Cry?

"We're here if you need us," Tony consoled, placing a hand on his shoulder.

Wayne nodded but was grateful when they left him alone. He sat at her side and took her slight hand in his.

"Hey, baby, it's me. Your shithead of a husband." He spoke and caressed her lifeless hand. Wayne wanted to shake her, do anything to wake her up.

The tears gathered in his eyes, and for the first time, the Beast felt fear and loneliness.

"I'd do anything for you to pull your hand away right now. To show me the woman you've become." He loosened his grip and waited to see if she'd pull away, but her hand remained still.

One tear fell from his eye and the ice around his heart smashed to smithereens. With Lily in his life, he had some semblance of control over his emotions. The thought of losing her and never seeing her smile, or even hearing her sing, was breaking him more than any gold digger could his bank balance.

A sob escaped, and he kissed her hand. Not caring about protocol, he lay down on the bed and gathered her in his arms.

"I know I'm a shit but don't leave me. I love you, Lily Jones. I've loved you from the first moment I saw you, even when you didn't see me. I'll love you till the day I die and then keep on loving you." The tears ran down his face. He didn't wipe them away. They were a beautiful thing. "Please, wake up. I want that family, and I've never been ashamed of you. I love you. I love you." He kissed the top of her head and held her tight. Any thoughts of keeping everything in his heart and remaining the bastard he'd become were gone. Lily could still be lost to him, but he'd keep telling her how much he loved her.

****

Tony and Richard came back with cups of coffee and saw their friend broken and sobbing in the neck of his wife.

"Wow, I never thought I'd see the Beast lose control like that," Richard said.

They moved out of the room and glanced through the slats in the window.

"He's in love, and it looks like the stupid asshole just realized what he could've lost by not telling her, too."

Richard frowned at his friend. "What do you know about love?"

Tony sighed and moved away from the heart-breaking scene. "The usual. I'm a bastard and let the girl get away...that kind of crap."

"Sounds a little cliché to me," Richard joked.

Both men had experienced love themselves, but neither was willing to talk about it. Watching Wayne almost lose his wife made them open their eyes to the bitterness within their own worlds. Maybe it was time for them to start finding love for themselves before ending up alone and bitter.

Chapter Eighteen

Someone was stroking her hair and whispering words of love in her ear. The sound kept fading, and she didn't know if she was imagining the sound.

"Come on, baby. Wake up. I love you." She knew that voice, but the fogginess in her mind couldn't place the soothing sound, or at least, she didn't accept what that particular voice was saying to her.

Her whole body ached and the pain in her chest the worst.

"Please, baby, come back to me."

No, I don't want to come with someone who doesn't love me.

Lily couldn't pretend any more. She opened her eyes and was immediately pulled to Wayne. Shaking, she allowed him to kiss and touch her but her heart wasn't there, but completely empty inside.

"They said you'd wake up eventually." He kissed her on the head, lips.

"Please stop," she asked, her voice hard.

Instantly, he withdrew from her. He lay on the bed wrapped around her. The heat radiated off him. Closing her eyes to contain herself, she took a deep breath before opening them. Lily needed the extra time to compose herself.

"I thought I'd lost you," he whispered.

His words and tenderness hurt even more, now he knew about the baby inside her, about the future heir she was carrying. All she ever wanted to do was get through this world with someone to love her. Her family hated her. For once she'd love to be someone's number one, to be the first thought on their mind.

"What happened?" she asked. Lily knew she lay in a hospital bed. She remembered the betrayal of his trust and her running out but everything after was a little fuzzy.

"After you left, you must have travelled through one of the roughest parts of the city. You were attacked, and witnesses said you were punched to the ground for your car. I should have been there."

Punched to the ground? It explained the massive headache she had. Why should he have been there? Wayne was the reason for her leaving the house in the first place.

"My turkey was in that car." She sobbed, the tears welling up from the uselessness of it all.

"We'll get another turkey." He stroked her face. All she wanted to do was lean toward his strength and take what he had to offer.

How pitiful was she? She was in love with a man who blackmailed her and hurt her by trying to force her to become something she didn't want. What was wrong with wanting to have a family?

"I don't want another turkey."

"What about our family? The baby?"

Lily closed her eyes remembering the pregnancy test she'd taken that morning, her gift for him. Her intention had been to have a lovely romantic meal before making love, and she planned to tell him her feelings about the new life growing inside her.

Instead, she came home to hell. It wasn't her home, not really. It was his.

"Wayne, I'm sorry to interrupt but someone's here." Lily turned toward the door to see Tony leaning around the private room. "Hi, Lily, how are you feeling?"

"Fine, like I've been punched," she said not bothering to smile.

"I'm going to go and see about this. Will you be okay on your own for a little while?" he asked.

"Of course, could you send Richard in? I want to ask him something." Lily couldn't look at him in case he knew what was in her mind.

"Yes, I'd do anything for you, baby. You should know that." He left seconds later, and Lily watched him go.

Why should she know that? Why should she even think he cared for her at all?

Lily pulled herself up into a sitting position, ran her fingers through her knotted hair. She wanted a shower and a toothbrush. She felt like absolute shit.

"You wanted to see me?" Richard came through the door and closed it behind him. She went to mess with her hair but stopped and glanced over at him.

Lily nodded. "I wanted to talk to you about the prenuptial agreement I signed."

He looked visually uncomfortable. Lily knew in her heart she wasn't going to like what was about to be discussed.

"I think this is something for you to discuss with Wayne," he suggested, edging closer to the door.

"Please, Richard, I'm asking you."

"I don't think I should tell you in your condition."

"You know I'm pregnant?"

"Wayne couldn't keep it to himself. He's very much in love with you." Lily snorted at the comment. She knew she shouldn't, but with all the revelations unravelling, she thought it was necessary to take facts head on.

"Just tell me what is going on." Lily rubbed a hand over her face, trying to clear her groggy thoughts. They stared at each other for several seconds before he nodded and looked everywhere but at her. Richard paced the small room.

"The prenuptial agreement is something Wayne has been drawing up for some time. I don't even know if I can tell you everything, but I'll try to give you the facts and the basics." He was nervous. Lily was sure of it now more than ever.

"Please, just tell me."

"Okay. Erm...right, the basis is the usual stuff—money, and securing his wealth in case of divorce, and settlement figures for you and your family in case of any long term problems that can't be fixed."

"He was going to pay me and my family off?"

"If this marriage didn't work out, you, in your own right would become a very wealthy woman but with the understanding you wouldn't use it on your family."

Lily smiled, touched by the sentiment of his caring.

"There's more. Wayne wanted you so badly...."

"Don't make excuses, just tell me."

"If there was a baby born during this union then Wayne automatically has sole custody and responsibility for the child and, indeed, for any other child born from this union."

"But I'm the mother."

"You signed your right away on the day you were married."

Lily lost her breath. The wind knocked out of her. Placing a hand against her neck, she tried to calm her nerves.

"Anything else," she asked.

Wayne would take her baby away.

"If at any time you wished to end your marriage, the child would stay with him, and you'd have supervised visits once a month for an hour. Also, if you divorced, you would remain attending to his wishes for the near future." Richard bit his lip, and Lily wiped the tears from her eyes.

"What do you mean?"

"The polite term would be remaining as his companion," he said.

"I'd be forced to be his whore!"

"I think that is a horrid term."

"Is there any way out of this contract?"

Richard shook his head. "I did warn you to get another lawyer to read it."

"And suffer the humiliation of what you've told me. Can a prenuptial agreement even contain stuff like this?" Her cheeks shined red from the shame.

"It's worded appropriately, and I believe Wayne never intended for it to get that far but as for it being possible, anything that can be written and verified can be placed in an agreement. I mean I think I read somewhere it was even illegal to eat a mince pie on Christmas day, somewhere." Lily knew he was trying to make light of the situation, but it didn't help.

"Please leave me alone. Thank you." She rolled over staring at the bland cream wall, wondering how many people had lain in the very same bed, broken-hearted and alone.

The tears fell, and she held her stomach.

"Wayne does love you."

The words failed to help. She didn't need anyone. She'd lived most of her life alone and she could continue to live for the sake of her child.

SAM CRESCENT

Chapter Nineteen

Wayne watched Richard enter his wife's room and thought about what she could want to discuss with the good man. He followed Tony to the waiting room. A nurse stood guarding a man.

"Mr. Brown, this gentleman refuses to leave."

He nodded for her to leave him, and he gave his full attention to George Jones, Lily's father.

The man looked pale and older since the last time he'd seen him, but after having Lily in his life, he didn't see the need getting in touch with the man who'd hurt her and risked thousands of people's jobs from his carelessness.

"What are you doing here, George?" He had no time to deal with spiteful families.

"I've just heard about Lily. Is she all right?" The older man pulled off his cap to reveal a full head of grey hair.

"As good as can be expected in her current condition."

Wayne was guarded. Her father, for the first time in all of her life, was taking notice of Lily.

"Thank God. I couldn't believe they wouldn't give me any information," he said exasperated, pointing at the reception desk.

"I'm her next of kin. I get to know everything."

"Can I see her?"

"You're responsible for making her life a fucking misery, and you expect me to let you see my wife who's been through enough already?" Wayne knew they were attracting attention but he no longer cared.

Fear and panic at the possibility of losing the woman he loved surfaced, and now, her snivelling shit of a father decided he wanted to be concerned, which just didn't cut it with him any longer. He was fucking sick of the falseness of dealing with it all.

"I love my daughter."

"Fuck you. You didn't love her. You practically threw her at me when the debt collectors started calling. Your family hate my fucking wife, and she's the nicest person to ever be born to shit like you. Now tell me why I shouldn't have you thrown on the street." Wayne knew how to deal. He may have been born around money, but he sure as shit made sure he could handle himself.

"Maybe we could go somewhere more privately to talk?"

"Come on, Wayne, you're really pushing it now," Tony said, taking his arm.

Wayne pulled out of his grip, squaring up to the older man.

"Tell me whatever I need to hear and then leave."

George stood floundering for a few minutes, finally nodding. Some years ago, twenty-two years to be precise, I had an affair with a sweet woman who came and worked as a cleaner for me in my London office at the time. You want all this. You can have it. A pretty woman only just out of her teens. She smiled at me and cleaned my desk, and one evening I took it upon myself to ask her out. I couldn't stop thinking about her—"

"Maybe we should take this somewhere private," Wayne interrupted. He spun round and moved to a private waiting area. "Continue."

"I've not thought about her in so long. I just shut it all out. Anyway, one thing led to another, and I slept with her, and we started a relationship. I know this sounds bad, but she thought I was just a manager of one of the departments. She didn't know I owned the place. It was a great business then, and I ruined it."

"Just get to it, George."

"She found out about my real name and my marriage, and everything blew up in my face. I loved her, not for her youth, or anything, I loved her. She was my heart and soul. I decided to screw the protocol of our standing and marry her. She was also pregnant with my child. I told Jessica I was leaving her, and everything was in place. Anyway, at some point, there were complications with her pregnancy, and I ended up taking her back home to where Jessica and Stephanie lived. I needed extra stuff to help care for her."

Wayne watched as George relived his moment of grief and unveiled the largest secret of the Jones's family.

"She gave birth in January. It was complicated, and we couldn't get her to the hospital. Snow and everything that comes with that shit. Lily was born, and her true mother bled out with no way of stopping. I can't remember what the doctors said. I was in shock. My Lily was gone."

Wayne frowned. "Your Lily?"

"Her name, the love of my life was called Lily. It was the only thing I fought Jessica on with her upbringing. She had to have the name Lily."

"Why did she live a shit life?"

"Because, Mr. Brown, I ceased to care about anything but the woman I lost. I stayed married to Jessica, and she cared for Lily but now I look back I see I was a horrid person. When Jessica told me to punish her, I did and I took my loss out on her. She didn't deserve the life I gave, but I was too blind." George allowed twenty-two years of contained tears to spill over.

"What happened for this change of heart?"

"I stood by the fire, burning some pictures from my wallet, and I picked one Jessica hadn't found of my Lily. I saw her adoring face so much like young Lily, and I woke up for the first time. My wife came in and handed me a sandwich and sneered that my whore's daughter was in hospital, and I finally snapped."

Wayne listened, understanding what he must have gone through. He only had to think of losing Lily, and it brought him to his knees.

"Let's just say I'm done. I don't want to be the monster of a man anymore. I loved Lily with all my heart, and instead of cutting it up and dealing, I should have loved the one thing that had been present of our love for each other—our child."

Wayne had two choices. Number one, send the man off and never allow him near his wife, or let Lily have something she truly needed.

"I want to warn you I love Lily with all my heart and soul. You do anything to fucking hurt her, and I'll fucking kill you."

George nodded and followed him to the spare room. Richard stood outside pacing and glanced at him as he walked closer.

Wayne let him go in and watched the scene unfold. Lily reached out for her father, and George went to her with open arms. He heard them talking and knew he'd made the right decision.

"She knows about the pre-nup, doesn't she?" Wayne asked a nervous Richard at his side.

"How do you know?"

"I know Lily, and I've fucked up. I want you to get every single copy of that...contract and bring it to me."

"All of it?"

"Everything."

Richard left him. Tony went to get more coffee, and Wayne got everything ready so he could take his wife home. Looking at the date on his watch, he noticed it was a week until Christmas. He wanted to make her first year with him special, but with all the ramifications rolling around, he truly believed everything he tried to do would be a lost cause.

Wayne watched the love of his life and prayed to the gods above to give him something to take away the Beast and bring her the man she deserved.

SAM CRESCENT

Chapter Twenty

They scattered around each other on tenterhooks. Lily worked at home, refusing to bring anyone else in to do the washing and the cooking. The two jobs she got pleasure from: cooking food and making her clothes clean. It was almost therapeutic.

Wayne stayed at home in either his office or following her around somewhere. He wouldn't leave her side no matter what she asked of him.

Her father came around as much as he could. He was working for Wayne, trying to build his life back up after the disaster of losing so much of his life already. George has given her a few diaries and keepsakes he kept hidden from her evil stepmother. The name still made her giggle. Knowing Jessica wasn't any relative of hers made her sleep easier at night and having Stephanie as a half-sister was easier to handle.

For a short while, she truly thought she'd end up like the spiteful duo that had gotten pleasure out of tormenting her.

The question she'd had for so long was answered: why everyone hated her. She was living proof of her father's love and infidelity with another woman. Lily took another item of clothing out and saw the lipstick mark on the neck of one of Wayne's shirts. After so long of being empty, the mark jolted something inside her. Closing her eyes, she tried to calm her nerves. It had been a few weeks since she'd done the washing. Disgusting, but after everything she hadn't got round to cleaning.

Screwing up the shirt, she put it on top of the machine and tried to blank out everything, to process her thoughts.

It doesn't mean anything.

Wayne is cheating on you!

It doesn't matter. I don't love him. I never have.

Oh really, so you call mourning his loss in bed at night and craving his attention and wishing just once he'd turn around and tell you how he felt, hating him?

This was ridiculous. Grabbing the shirt, she charged down to his office. The door was shut, as usual before lunch.

Turn back around and pretend it doesn't mean anything.

Nonsense, go in and confront him. Be a woman and take matters in your own hands.

Two voices were arguing amongst themselves. The child and the adult.

A child would skulk off and let it be. A woman would fight for her love.

Did she love him?

Do I have to do everything for you? Why do you think it hurts so damn much? You're breaking inside, pregnant with his child and all you want is to be loved. Go in there and get him, tiger.

Nodding, she put her hand on the doorknob and froze.

More pain, is that what you want? Voice number two whispered along her brain.

Lily prayed. Other women had these moments, otherwise she was putting herself in a sealed room with lots of fucking padding.

Lily jumped back as she opened the door. She screamed and tripped over, landing on her back.

"Lily!" Wayne took her in his arms and escorted her into his study, placing her gently down on the sofa she'd put in for his comfort. "I don't want you hurting yourself. Why didn't you just come in?"

"Hurting myself or the baby?" she growled.

Wayne jerked as if she'd burnt him with her words.

"Never mind, forget I ever said anything." Lily moved out from under him. Having him so close and not thinking about touching him was too difficult to process.

"Lily, wait."

"You know I don't want to do this." She flapped her hands above her head and moved away.

"Lily?"

"Actually, you know what I think. I'm sick, Wayne. I'm sick of you and everything you stand for." Lily had no idea what she was saying, but she kept on. "You blackmail me with family that isn't even mine to become your wife. I don't even know you all that well! I have no honeymoon besides the cottage trip, which was lovely, but then you blurt out about the baby and that heavy contract and now all this and...and...." Lily took the shirt, stormed over to him, slapped him on the cheek, and pressed the lipstick mark right up in his face.

"What's this? Another one of your floozies?"

"Lily, you're not making sense."

"Don't give me one of your excuses. The shirt has lipstick on it. I don't wear make-up, shithead."

"You just called me shithead?"

"Yeah, and I'll call you worse before the end of the day. I won't have you...." Whatever she was about to say stopped as his lips took possession of her mouth, melting the coldness and shooting a spark to her heat.

Lily moaned and dropped the shirt to the floor. Her breasts ached, and her cunt was swimming for more of this man and his hard cock.

She stopped. Shit, she'd given in too soon. Pulling out of his arms, she shot him a fierce look, wiping her mouth.

Wayne picked his shit from the floor and looked at the lipstick. "It's your sister's."

Lily saw red. How many other women would brush off a statement like that?

She charged at him, lashing out, and punching his chest. Her hormones were out of whack.

"Listen to me," Wayne ordered. He grabbed her hands and thrust her up against the nearest wall. "Your sister came to my office and tried to seduce me. Do you think for the world I would fuck a bag of bones when I have you here and wanting me?"

Lily struggled against his hold. His leg inserted between her thighs rubbing the folds of her sensitive flesh.

Biting off a moan, she tried to concentrate on what he was saying.

"But she got lipstick on you."

"The woman practically attacked me, but don't worry, my cock only gets hard for one woman, and she's squirming under me right now."

In one swift move, he tore her dress from tit to waist. Her breasts bare, as the bras she used to wear hurt too damn much.

Wayne cupped her breasts, and she moaned. The cool air delightful on the heated nubs.

"This is the woman I want. I love you, Lily." He growled as he took a nipple with his lips.

Lily jolted. "What? What did you say?"

"I love you, Lily, always have and always will."

He didn't give her time to think about what he'd said, instead he showed her. Their clothes went in a heap on the floor. He took her up against the wall, his cock thrusting inside her, taking her to newfound heights of completion. Next on the sofa, where she rode him, their climax fast and furious. Lily couldn't get enough of his cock, and they lay panting in a mass on the sofa.

"I love you, Lily," he said again, kissing her shoulder and moving her hair out of the way.

"How do you know?" She shivered from his touch, her body tingling all over from an afternoon of rigorous sex.

"Some time ago you were at a ball, nineteen, one of the few times I'd seen you attend. I knew back then."

"But you're older than me."

"Do you really think this has anything to do with age?" He touched his heart and touched her breast.

"You're trying to distract me." Lily arched up to his touch.

"Lily, I love you with all my heart." He went serious on her, and she knew in that moment, he was telling the truth.

"But everything you've done?"

"Look. I've got shitloads to tell you about my life."

"Then tell me."

Wayne glanced at her, and Lily sent him a smile.

"Okay. For some time, I've been on my own. My family are monsters, Lily. I was born to two people who are more selfish than the whole world put together."

"That's a bit extreme." Lily could see the emotion breaking through the blocks of ice and walls he'd erected around himself. Is it possible he was protecting himself from hurt? The very Beast himself had a weakness?

"That's the problem with our world. It's either one extreme or the other. We don't do stuff like half measures." He licked his lips and cupped her cheek. "As a young boy, my parents...they...." He couldn't finish, and Lily got the message loud and clear.

"They hurt you." There was so much more to this man than a big cock and reputation. A broken child lay beneath the surface, lost and alone exactly like her.

"Yes." He sobbed. Tears formed in his eyes, and she watched in total amazement as the man who was always in control, brutal in his approach, weakened before her.

Lily caressed his cheeks and stared in wonder as the tears spilled. She leaned down and kissed them away.

"I'm a horrible man. I've hurt you more than I've ever hurt anyone else." His large hands encircled her waist and held her close. His head nuzzled her bosom as he let the sobs release. Lily held him, consoled him.

"I've got you," she whispered, stroking his hair back from his face. Her breasts were coated with his tears. After some time, he stopped.

Wayne looked up, about to talk, but she stopped him with a finger over his lips. "You don't need to tell me. I understand, and thank you for giving me some of yourself already." She kissed him on the lips.

"I want to show you something." Wayne picked her up, placed her on the sofa, and went to his desk.

Lily recognized the contract she'd signed in Richard's office, and her heart beat rapidly in her chest.

"Why do you have that awful thing?"

"Because I want to give you every copy that was ever made." He handed her the paper copies and a disk. "That is everything linking to that contract. As far as I'm concerned, you're my wife by choice not by contract."

"What if I walk out of here?" Lily tested him.

"Then my heart will go with you wherever you want to go, but I'll warn you now: you'll never find a man out there who'll love you the way I do."

Lily watched him freeze. He stared at her, but his hands fisted at his sides. Getting to her feet with the contract in her hands, she walked over the fireplace and threw the documents and disk onto the fire. The paper went up in flames, and the plastic began to melt.

Her heart lifted in her chest.

"Why did you do that?"

"Because I don't need any contract to tell me how I feel. For some strange reason, Wayne Brown, I've fallen deeply in love with you, and I can forgive everything you've done, and everything you're going to end up doing to me. I forgive you."

Lily walked over to him and hugged him tight. They stood naked in front of the fire, the heat radiating to them. Wayne put his arms around her waist. She giggled when his cock bumped her back.

"Someone's pleased to see me."

"I'll always be pleased to see you, baby," Wayne said, nuzzling her neck. "I'm going to do something I should have done at the very beginning."

Lily stood while Wayne moved to his clothing. He came back to her and went on one knee. "Lily Jones, the light of my life, the love of my life. I'll love you forever with my heart, mind, body, and soul. I've been an utter bastard, but I do love you with everything that I am. Will you make this *Beast* whole and become my wife?"

As far as marriage proposals go, it was the most beautiful she'd ever witnessed. Nodding, she accepted the new ring he presented her with.

****

A few days before Christmas, Lily Jones, who was once blackmailed by a beast, was suddenly the very reason for him to open up and become the man willing to love her, and she willing to love the man with all of her heart.

Epilogue

Richard smiled at the text message from his recent conquest. An amateur model from some fashion show who did a really nice trick with her mouth. She sucked his dick like a lollipop.

It was his lunch break, and he'd already seen Lily and Wayne. They wanted him to be a godparent slash uncle for their unborn son. She'd had the ultrasound confirming sex, and they were already planning a room and decorations. Seeing the love and happiness in his friends' faces gave him a shred of hope. Even though the Beast was still very much present in negotiations, people noticed a difference in him.

Some people were just made for each other.

Glancing out of his office window, he watched Scarlet Hughes, the young office trainee fresh out of college and a thorn in his ever-loving side, bend over the desk. Her rounded ass was in full view and his dick tented in his trousers. Fucking hell, he was a thirty-year-old man. He did not lust after young women.

There was nothing wrong with the girl other than his growing attraction to her. Everyone in the office adored her. She was so lovable and baked cookies for everyone, even the clients enjoyed her calming presence.

Shaking his head at the horrid, inappropriate thoughts running through his head, he sent back a text to his overindulgent and older flavour of the month.

Want some loving. U available 2night?

Richard knew he'd never get the hang of text talk. He was a lawyer for Christ's sakes. He shouldn't be using abbreviations for anything but case law and legislation with note taking.

A knock on the door disrupted his thoughts. Scarlet stood waiting for his call. Turning his phone onto vibrate, he gestured for her to enter.

"You've got mail here, and I've been told to tell you, your two o'clock is running behind." She handed him the letters and the note slip.

Scarlet turned to leave, and Richard enjoyed the view of her ass. Not a skinny thing that he usually liked but a nice plump bottom. He thought how tasty it would be to bite into the rounded flesh.

Fuck. Pre-cum was already leaking from his slit. He could feel the damn thing.

"Oh, before I forget," she said, turning back to face him. "I noticed your friends earlier. Please let me not make a fool of myself but the woman is pregnant right?"

"You mean Lily? Yes, she's pregnant." He pulled himself farther under the desk, hoping she wouldn't see his tight trousers.

"Well, I've got a cot and pram. I know some people like to buy new but these have been well-looked after, and I'd love to see them go to a new home."

"You've got a child?"

"Yes, Harry, he's four in August." She came forward, pulling out a mobile phone. Even to him, the thing looked dated. She showed him a picture of a young boy.

"How old are you?"

"I'm twenty-two, sir."

This was so wrong. The woman he lusted after had a child of four.

"I think they'll buy new," he said and stopped when he saw the disappointment on her face.

"Oh, yes, I understand. Thanks anyway."

She moved out of the office, and he could breathe easier. He steered away from women with kids. Why would she be any different?

Unfortunately, Richard didn't have an answer for that question.

The End

www.samcrescent.wordpress.com

Evernight Publishing

www.evernightpublishing.com

www.ingramcontent.com/pod-product-compliance
Lightning Source LLC
Chambersburg PA
CBHW022033170626
46808CB00003B/1178